Cover Illustration by Julie Bonart of Qamber Designs
Cover layout & typography by Qamber Designs
Editing by Jessica Snyder

UNHITCHED

PIPPA GRANT WRITING AS
JAMIE FARRELL

*B*en Garcia flipped his shades down, popped the top on a cold beer, and surveyed the wide street a block off the beach in Coconut Bay. Beach bums, locals, and tourists lined either side of the main drag. He could tell who'd been to the water parade before and who hadn't based on the size of their Super Soakers and the flavor of their tan.

The women huddled half a block up with squirt guns the size of an ant, trying to hide behind a stop sign in front of Flip Flops Beach Emporium?

First-time tourists.

The frat guys dragging a flat wagon with two fifty-gallon drums of water and a stock of water cannons, pushing a family out of the way to claim a spot at the start of the bend in the road twenty feet away?

Repeat tourists.

The old dudes hanging out on the roof of the deceptively run-down looking Janie Mae's Oyster Bar, where none of the tourists had noticed them yet, making them relatively safe from early shots with the water cannons?

Locals.

There'd be more locals coming on the floats that were behind the lead-off fire truck, which was also visible about four blocks down, because the locals always knew the best spot to enjoy the annual water parade.

Ben supposed he counted as a local. His mother had moved here five years ago, and he himself had been here an entire fifteen months. And three weeks and two days, but who was counting?

"Ben! Bennie! There you are!" Nikita Fleming bounced to a stop beside his old lawn chair, her assets jiggling in her pink bikini. Her hair was platinum, her tan a testament to her dedication to being ready for the June sun coming next week, her eyes hidden by sunglasses that ate half her face. She squatted beside him and flashed him a blinding smile, which was appropriate, considering she was the town's only dentist. "Your mom said I'd find you here."

He nodded to her and offered her a beer.

Her nose wrinkled. "That's disgusting."

He didn't disagree. Tasted like watered down barley bubbles. But beach town festivities called for light beer in cans, and he was doing his part to embrace the beach lifestyle.

Plus, glass bottles were prohibited at the water parade. Too easily broken if the water fights got out of hand.

A teenager sprinted past firing a water cannon at them, and Nikita took a hit right in the chest, while Ben got a misty spray on his shoulder. She squealed, unearthed a Super Soaker, spun, and nailed the kid in the back.

How it went in the annual water fight.

"Here." She reached into her turquoise-and-pink striped beach bag and pulled out three dripping water cannons. "You shouldn't be out here unarmed. Remember last year? If they know you're unarmed, they won't stop."

"Thanks, Mom," he said dryly.

Nikita swatted his arm. "Stop. You *know* I'm not your mom."

He knew very well what Nikita wanted to be.

And he also knew very well that the point of the water parade was to get wet. Which was the more immediate situation to deal with.

He was embracing this. Dammit. He'd get wet, and he'd like it.

He spent just about every day on the beach himself.

Of course he'd get wet and like it.

"I'm not your mom either." Chloe Ashley appeared at his other side. She was Nikita's opposite—brown hair, pale skin, covered in not just a one-piece black swimsuit, but also wrapped in a colorful sarong, her arms covered with a see-through white button-down, her hair shielded with the biggest straw hat in Florida, and her eyes hidden by normal-size sunglasses with leopard-print rims. "But I brought you sunscreen and a jug of water for refills."

The frat guys noticed Ben, Nikita, and Chloe, and turned loose sixteen water cannons, drenching all three of them.

Nikita fired back with her Super Soaker. Chloe hauled out the water cannon to end all water cannons, let out a high-pitched war screech, and unloaded on the frat guys until they turned their attention to easier targets.

Ben let the women take the lead in the battle and took another pull off his beer.

Once that threat had been neutralized, Chloe pulled out the promised gallon jug from her beach bag and plopped it at his feet, giving him a view of ample cleavage. She was a real estate agent by day, number two on his mother's preferred list of women he should date by night.

Right in front of Nikita

Whom his mother disapproved of on the grounds that she'd die of skin cancer before she was forty-five, most likely leaving him a single father who would once again need a parade of women to fill the void in his life. But Nikita stayed on the list, because at least Mom would get a good twelve or fifteen years of a break between matchmaker stints if Ben was able to successfully resist her attempts to match him with candidates one and two.

Which so far, he'd done spectacularly well.

Had to be good at something, didn't he?

"Benji! Silly, why are you hiding back here?"

And there was his mother's top candidate for Ben's love life. Emmanuelle Genevieve Jones-Beaumont, heiress to the soft serve ice cream empire in Coconut Bay.

Emmanuelle—whom no one dared to call Emmy—came with an old-fashioned dowry that included three ice cream stands, a snack bar on the boardwalk, and a Victorian mansion on the only hill in Coconut Bay, which gave it the distinct advantage of also having the best view of the sunsets over the gulf.

Yep.

Emmanuelle was a catch.

But Ben wasn't fishing.

Not like his mother was.

Even if Emmanuelle's black and white polka-dot two-piece with boy shorts showcased all of her curves nicely and left little to the imagination.

The body didn't make up for the pitfalls.

And the number one pitfall was the voice in the back of Ben's head whispering that he knew exactly how to turn Emmanuelle's family's ice cream franchise into a nationwide success with corporate offices in all quadrants of the country.

Didn't matter how much that itch itched. He wasn't selling his soul to corporate America again, and he wasn't marrying a woman just to get back into business.

He was looking for a smaller job. Something more grounded. More connected to people.

Nikita, Chloe, and Emmanuelle gathered around his chair, offering hints and tricks to staying dry or getting the most people wet during the water parade while occasionally defending their turf from water attacks. The first fire truck was lumbering closer up Palm Street, shooting bystanders with fire hoses.

The old dudes on top of Janie Mae's had discreetly ducked back inside, because it was well-known in Coconut Bay that no one

4

outdoors escaped the wrath of the lead fire truck in the water parade.

"Did that woman find you?" Emmanuelle asked him suddenly. They were all pretty wet by now, and Ben was on his second watered-down beer.

He shifted his gaze between Chloe, whose hat was drooping, and Nikita. "They both did."

"No, Benji," she said with a smile that suggested she didn't think anything of calling him a dog's name, "the beanpole who missed the memo about the water parade."

So his mother had found a fourth candidate.

Wonderful.

He supposed he should be grateful she picked women who didn't seem to mind that they were in competition with each other. Nikita, Chloe, and Emmanuelle all got along pretty well. They'd all told him at one time or another that either life was too short to be bitchy—that was Nikita—that the town was too small for catfights over someone who might not stick around—Chloe—or that there was no sense in getting jealous when she knew she'd get him in the end anyway —Emmanuelle.

Emmanuelle was wrong—he'd given up running empires fifteen months, three weeks, and two days ago, and he wasn't doing it again, even if three ice cream stands and a snack bar on the boardwalk were a far cry from the empires he'd run in his previous life.

Empires were still empires, and stress was still stress.

And he still knew himself well enough to know that as soon as he dipped one toe in, he'd go from swimming to drowning in under a year.

He didn't half-ass anything.

Though he was starting to wish he could half-ass being a beach bum. Life was getting boring.

"You feeling okay, Bennie?" Nikita leaned into his space, giving him a view of *her* cleavage and the water dripping down her bronze skin. "You're awful quiet today."

5

"He doesn't need to talk," Chloe interjected. "He has us for that. Who's the beanpole? Your mama knows we don't share with tourists, and I can't think of anyone I know that I'd call a beanpole."

"She looked like she could've been coming from Orlando or Gainesville," Emmanuelle said. "On official business. Definitely not a tourist. But she's not local either."

"Like from a law office?" Nikita wanted to know. "Bennie, you don't have a secret love child floating around you haven't told us about, have you?"

"Foreclosed on a property in California?" Emmanuelle guessed.

"Have a long-lost great-uncle who died and needs to find you as his sole heir?" Chloe suggested.

The fire truck's horn blared. It was just a block away now, and the shrieks were getting louder. The frat boys were firing their water cannons at a group of middle-aged women who were firing back with a hose someone had pulled out from behind Diego's T-Shirt Shack.

Ben forced a smile and a wink at the three women who were staring at him expectantly. Maybe he should take tomorrow off. Go deep sea fishing with his buddy Krill.

Suggest Krill go ask Ben's mom out on another date, because she hated when Ben turned the tables on her, and, in her own words, Krill was too old for her.

"Don't have a clue who she is," he told the women.

All three visibly relaxed.

For a split second.

Until they were attacked by a family with sixteen kids under ten, all armed with baby water pistols. Ben shot back with lazy bursts out of his water cannon that all went over their heads. Nikita shrieked and pretended the kids were getting her wetter than they were, and that she was out of water in her Super Soaker. Chloe's water cannon jammed—or so she said—and Emmanuelle fired back with rubber duckies that shot water out of their mouths.

The fire truck turned the corner, its hose soaking everyone and everything in a twenty-yard radius with a rain of water. Ben's hair was dripping in his eyes, his chest was cold, and his beer can really *was* half-water now.

Yep.

This was what living felt like. Getting soaked on the corner of a beach town during the biggest party of the year.

Once the fire truck had passed, everyone scattered to refill their water shooters. The frat guys ran their fifty-gallon drums to a hose beyond one of the pastel-painted souvenir shops. Families and tourists and strangers shared water jugs. And a beanpole poked her head out of Sunny's Island Trinkets and looked up and down the street.

Ben straightened. He dropped his beer can.

And his heart—that ticking time bomb that had led him to Coconut Bay—tripped, picked itself up, and sprinted into overdrive.

Her green eyes connected with his, and fragments of a memory erupted in Technicolor beneath the electric hum that buzzed through the air between them.

Neon lights.

Elvis.

Rumpled sheets.

Laughter.

So much laughter.

She pulled herself straight—still tall, still slender—and her eyes—which had widened in recognition—now narrowed in determination.

His heart was pounding so fast he was going lightheaded.

Shit. *Shit.*

She adjusted the strap of her cotton satchel and stepped out of the shop, eyes still locked on his, her steps confident and deliberate. She was in casual khaki pants and a flowery, ruffled top, sandals that weren't water shoes, with a single bracelet dangled from her slender wrist at the end of her long arm. Her brown hair was tied back at her neck, with wispy flyaways dancing in the breeze around her head, touching her high cheekbones.

He should stand up.

Say something.

Greet her.

But he couldn't make himself move.

She was Vegas.

Not Coconut Bay.

He sensed Nikita, Chloe, and Emmanuelle closing ranks two seconds too late.

"Ben," Tarra Blue said.

And before she could say another word, his mother's top three favorite women unloaded on her.

Nikita got her with the Super Soaker that wasn't out of water. Chloe didn't hold back with the water cannon. And Emmanuelle hefted a five-gallon bucket and swung it expertly to completely coat Tarra from head to foot in beach water.

Ben scrambled to his feet. "Stop!"

His mother's chosen three swung matching *oh, no, you didn't* gazes on him.

"You come to the water parade, you get wet," Emmanuelle said in a tone he hadn't heard before.

The *who the hell do you think you are?* tone.

"And you already have three of us," Chloe added.

"We're not doing this with one more," Nikita agreed. "Especially not a stranger."

Tarra was soaked.

Head to toe.

Her hair was dripping. Makeup running. Ruffled flower shirt plastered to her chest.

God, that chest.

It'd been ten years, and he still remembered that chest.

Not because she was stacked—quite the opposite.

But because her breasts had been so responsive to his every touch.

She picked at the shirt and tried to pull it off her body, where it was sticking to every curve.

"I'm sorry," she said to the three women, not sounding sorry in the least, "but it appears we've gotten off on the wrong foot."

She smiled, a remarkably non-smiley smile, which was sad, because her smile and her laugh—those had stayed with him more days than he could count.

"Who are you, and what do you want with our Bennie?" Nikita demanded.

"I'm Tarra," she answered, "and I'm Ben's wife."

*a*s in all things this year, Tarra Blue had terrible timing.

She'd gotten pregnant before her wedding.

She'd found out she was accidentally still married literally two seconds before she was supposed to walk down the aisle.

And when she'd finally found her husband—the man who was supposed to be her *ex*-husband—she'd found him in the middle of the wettest parade on earth.

With his harem.

Who were all remarkably strong with remarkably good aim.

It took a hell of a lot of strength to throw five gallons of water like that. She'd have to watch out for polka-dot bikini chick.

"Sorry about that," Ben said for the seventeenth time since he'd hustled her off the main street and down a side road that—luckily—was on the same side of the parade route as the condo she'd rented for the next two nights. "Any other day—"

"Your harem wouldn't have been gunning for me?" she guessed lightly as she pulled her infuser out of her tea mug in the small kitchen of her temporary digs.

He ran a hand through his dark, wet curls.

He should've put a shirt on. Because having him standing here in this airy, beach-themed condo in wet board shorts that clung to his solid thighs was distraction enough without the addition of the broad, hard chest, flat stomach, and tapered hips.

She'd forgotten he had an outie.

And clearly pregnancy hormones were screwing with her head, because she wanted to touch it.

She hadn't seen him in ten years, not since they decided—okay, *he* decided—that their quickie Vegas wedding had been a mistake and they filed for a divorce before they both went their separate ways, and she wanted to touch—okay, fine, *lick*—his belly button.

"Despite what it looked like—" he started.

She waved him quiet. "Oh, please. You don't owe me any explanations. We're supposed to be divorced. *Not* married."

"We're not—"

"Oh, we are. The attorney in Vegas never filed the paperwork. Which we can resolve immediately. I have divorce papers in my bag. We can sign them today, I'll fax them back to my lawyer, and you can get back to harem-ing it up."

The idea of Ben Garcia getting busy with three women shouldn't have bothered her. He wasn't *hers*. Not in any sense beyond the *what happens in Vegas stays in Vegas* kind of way.

His dark brown eyes were trained on her, but she got the feeling he wasn't *seeing* her.

She got the feeling he wasn't thinking about a foursome with the formidable women who'd ambushed her outside the cute little beach souvenir shop either. His breath was entirely too steady, and if she was a guy thinking about doing it with three women, there would be not only some shortness of breath, but also some movement in her pants.

His wet board shorts made it distinctly obvious that part of his anatomy wasn't involved in his thoughts.

"You're sure you don't want any tea?" she offered.

He blinked twice, gripped his hair again, and shook his head. "Are you sure we're still married?"

"Want to hear about my fiancé leaving me at the altar when his mother's PI turned up with the news at the very last second?" she offered cheerfully.

He winced. "Ouch."

"It's not so bad," she countered. Because it had been two months since the break-up, and lots of meditation, tea, and kickboxing had helped her forgive herself for being so desperate to believe she was happy that she almost saddled herself to the Prince of Dicks for the rest of her life. "There's a bright side to everything. And it's your lucky day, because I've already taken care of getting new divorce papers drawn up. All you have to do is sign. Unless you want your attorney to look at them. But since we never combined assets and we both thought we already *were* divorced, it's all very simple."

This was so surreal. She'd come here to get a divorce from a guy she barely knew, but standing here, watching him watch her, she felt like a stranger in her own life.

Was getting married in Vegas something she regretted?

Not really. You only live once, he'd been entertaining, and sure, they'd gotten carried away after winning a thousand bucks on a slot machine, but *god*, that weekend had been fun.

Even with the quickie divorce, she hadn't harbored any ill will toward him.

He'd had some big corporate job to get back to in California, and even if she'd hated her desk job filing paperwork for a government contractor near St. Louis ten years ago, before she'd finally found what she was supposed to do with her life, she'd loved living near family and hadn't wanted to move out West, so far from her sisters and nieces and the rest of her family.

They were friends who connected immediately and got carried away.

And had some amazing sex.

Nope.

No regrets.

But it was time they were both legally free.

She blew on her tea. Lemon mango had seemed an appropriate choice for the beach. Plus, she wanted the warmth. The air conditioning in here was frigid, and though she'd changed into dry pants and another loose top—the better to hide her rapidly growing baby bump—her hair was still wet.

Even the little heater in her belly wasn't helping the shiver slinking over her skin.

Ben was thinking again.

She didn't remember him thinking this much in Vegas.

He'd been fun. Flirty. Smiley.

Maybe a little high-strung too, but nobody was perfect.

She carried her unicorn mug toward the sliding door to the third-story porch outside the condo's kitchen, since turning the thermostat up wasn't helping quickly. "Papers are on the coffee table," she told him. "I'll be outside enjoying the fresh air."

She wouldn't have much more time for beach getaways once she was done here.

And then when the baby was born, she'd have even less.

Not that she planned on giving up travel. It would just be a while before the baby would be old enough to be slathered in sunscreen and trusted not to eat sand.

She settled into the weather-worn stiff cushion over a wicker chair on the small porch, propping her feet on the funky brown wicker coffee table. The air was salty, and though she couldn't hear the Gulf of Mexico rolling onto the shore just a block away, she could watch the sun dance and sparkle on the waves and follow the deep blue all the way to the horizon.

Tomorrow she'd go on a dolphin tour.

After she made sure everything was running fine back at work.

Laughter drifted up from the street. The parade was over, but the water fights apparently still raged on. She sipped her tea, closed her eyes, and sighed.

She hadn't expected her own investigator to discover Ben on *this* coast. Or to report that he'd been unemployed for the last year or so.

She'd honestly expected to arrive here, meet some other Ben Garcia—hardly an uncommon name—who wasn't the Ben she'd married, and go home to tell her investigator to start over.

But this was definitely the Ben she'd married. The dark hair, the dark eyes.

The spark.

Even if the rest of him seemed different.

The sliding door whooshed open, and she pried her eyelids open to watch him slip out onto the porch.

He sat at the edge of the chair beside her. No papers. No shirt.

He looked out at the ocean too.

But only briefly before turning to look her in the eye. "What if we didn't get divorced?"

3

*B*en knew exactly three things about Tarra Blue.

One, she was still as pretty as the day he'd met her. Prettier, if that was possible.

Two, she still rolled with the punches. *Oh. Well, if you're not sure, then yeah, I guess we'll leave us in Vegas. But I'll always remember you fondly.*

And three, she could very well be the ticket to his mother laying the hell off with the matchmaking.

She peered at him with those exotic green eyes over a white mug with a cartoon unicorn printed on it. "I'm sorry, I must still have some water in my ears, because I thought you just said—"

"You're not wearing a ring."

She lifted her left hand, eyed her long, slender, lavender-tipped fingers, and she wrinkled her nose.

So apparently she did have a feather or two that could be ruffled.

Barely.

She hadn't blinked when he'd said *it's a sign, let's get married* ten years ago when she'd been the good luck charm that had won him a grand at a slot machine—pocket change for him in those days.

Nor had she blinked when he'd said *this might've been a mistake* two days later.

"You still with—what was his name?" he asked.

More nose wrinkling.

She wasn't with him.

"Meet someone else?" he asked.

She did one of those loaded eye rolls. Like there was a long story there that ended with *most definitely not*. But her eye roll also ended with a warm smile. "I don't do sister-wives," she informed him.

"Too bad. I think Chloe was into you."

"Was she the one with the bucket?"

"The water cannon."

She sipped her tea thoughtfully. "Funny. I got the threesome vibe more from the chick in the pink bikini."

He opened his mouth, then closed it again when her grin sparkled to life. She set her mug down and straightened. "It's very noble of you to try to save me from the indignity of a divorce, but I have faith we can handle this like two rational adults."

"I missed you."

Shit, where had that come from?

Tarra fluttered a hand again. "You missed the fun. *I* missed the fun. And it was fun to have a person for a while, but we—"

"Had a lot of fun," he finished quietly, because he didn't want to hear her say *weren't right for each other*.

She wasn't wrong.

He'd missed the fun.

But he'd had flings with other women throughout the years.

And he'd never had the *fun*.

Or the insane desire to ask another woman to marry him hours after they met.

Did that say something about him? About her? Or about *them*?

He smiled at the concrete patio floor. "I'd never been skinny dipping in a hotel pool before," he confessed.

"I still haven't made it to Venice for a real gondola ride."

"Had any more six-course chocolate meals?"

She laughed. "Had to go there, didn't you?"

"You were adorable bent over the toilet like that."

"I didn't have another piece of chocolate for *two years*. I was *very* popular with my sisters back then, because they got all my desserts whenever we were together."

Her sisters. He remembered stories about her sisters. "All ten of them?"

She tilted her head at him, her brows momentarily furrowing before she turned and reached for her tea again. "No, only eight of them. Margie was on one of her *caffeine is bad for the human body* kicks, and Sage had just read something about working conditions in cacao fields and refused for humanitarian reasons." She took a small sip and met his eyes again. "You remembered I have ten sisters."

"Hard to forget something that terrifying." He was an only child, but that didn't mean he was unfamiliar with women. He'd heard his share of sister horror stories.

She laughed and leaned back again, cradling her tea. She had such fine features. The upturned nose. The hollow in her cheeks. The delicate spread of her collarbones. Her small breasts, hidden under another ruffle shirt.

"My mother wants me to get married," he blurted.

Because he was apparently smooth moves and all the right words with Tarra Blue.

Which was the complete opposite of how he'd been ten years ago, when they'd had their Vegas fling.

She sipped her tea again, clearly mulling over the information. "So being already married is quite convenient for you."

He shrugged. Tried for nonchalant. Probably looked more like lazy bum.

A lazy beach bum.

That's what he was.

What he was trying to be, anyway.

"It's not *inconvenient*," he clarified.

17

She opened her mouth, but whatever she was going to say was drowned out by a racket that exploded from the third-floor condo unit of the building next door.

A tall woman.

In her early sixties.

With her silver hair custom-colored and cut short, jewels on every finger, a stud in her nose, and a locket with his baby picture hanging around her neck.

Which he knew, because the racket was his mother.

It wasn't even her condo, but then, Coconut Bay was small, and she'd no doubt gotten herself an easy invitation to the balcony over there.

"Benjamin Anthony Garcia, *when were you going to introduce me to your wife?*"

Tarra's eyes drifted between him and his mother, who had almost certainly been in touch with Nikita, Chloe, and Emmanuelle. Or any number of other people out at the water parade.

Word traveled fast in places like this.

His mom waved and blew a kiss at Tarra. "Hello, dear. I'm Betty. Come closer. I need a good look at the woman who stole my son's heart so good *he didn't even tell me about her.*"

Ben sighed.

Tarra quirked a brow at him. "You voluntarily gave up a cushy job in California to move closer to your mother?"

Apparently her PI had gotten her a lot more dirt on him than he had on her.

This didn't bode well for negotiations for staying married.

Or for a quick excuse for his mother to quit her scheming and matchmaking.

"Long story," he said.

"Come over for dinner," his mom called. "I put a lasagna in the oven. Lots of meat and cheese. It'll fatten you up in no time. Then we can talk about how old you are and how soon you'll be giving me grandbabies."

Tarra stiffened, but she covered it with another sip of tea. "Must be some story."

He sighed.

She wasn't going to go for staying married.

And why should she? He was a guy who lived with his mother, didn't have a real job, and couldn't even say out loud why he'd left the corporate world behind, even if most of the Coconut Bay locals had spent the first six months of his time here whispering about it behind his back.

She leaned over and patted his knee. The press of her fingers on his skin sent a jolt through his body.

When he'd left Vegas ten years ago, he'd told himself that the feeling of leaving a part of himself behind was regret over the hasty marriage and divorce.

It had been easier to accept than wondering if he'd let the woman of his dreams get away.

"Come on then," she said, rising to her feet. "You're going to have to explain one way or another. Might as well get it over with."

He jerked his head up. "What?"

"I've already done the *so I got married in Vegas this one time* story with my own family. Four times, actually, because—anyway. I've got it down. I'm here. Might as well break it to your mother the easy way. And I love a good lasagna."

He did too.

And his mother might not have a quiet, not-nosy bone in her body, but she could cook.

Tarra waved to his mother. "Hi, Betty. I'm Tarra. And we'd love to come to dinner. What time?"

"Ten minutes," his mom called back.

"Give us fifteen," she replied with a wink that probably made his mother's entire life.

He jumped up and followed Tarra into the kitchen. "Can't go anywhere without getting soaked tonight. The water fights go on until dark."

"Good thing my rental car has windows that close."

He stopped her against the counter, not meaning to trap her, but as soon as his body came into contact with hers—firmer than he remembered, with more curves too—he didn't want to move away. "So we're staying married."

She pushed at his chest, and sensations danced over his skin like hurricane waves sweeping over sand. "We're still getting divorced. But I'm here until Sunday night, and I'm hungry, and I'm really hoping your mother's the type to pull out baby pictures, because we've been married for ten years. I should've seen baby pictures by now."

This was unexpected.

And not at all reassuring.

His wife could apparently steamroll with the best of them.

God help his mother.

4

*S*o maybe dinner with Ben's mother wasn't Tarra's best idea ever. It certainly wasn't orthodox.

But her best idea ever—dating and getting engaged to Jack—had ended in utter disaster.

Not that being pregnant was a disaster. She was *thrilled* about being pregnant. At thirty-eight, she'd thought she'd never be a mother, yet here she was, in her second trimester, with the baby growing strong and healthy and right on track.

Yes, things could get ugly if Jack decided to lawyer up and sue for visitation rights, but he'd walked away. He'd known she was pregnant, and he still walked away.

Like he was relieved to be escaping the noose of marriage and fatherhood.

She'd never be that blind again. Never put *wanting* to be loved over actually *being* loved.

But she wasn't cruel either, and she knew first-hand how shocking it was to find out a marriage she'd thought had been permanently undone and erased was actually still legally in existence.

So if having a sit-down with Ben's mother to explain the situation would make things easier for him, she'd do it.

And she really did like lasagna.

As did the baby, apparently.

"Anything in particular I should know about your mother?" she asked Ben while they drove what he called *the back way* to his mother's house. People were still milling about with water toys, and he had to keep wiping the windshield to be able to see through the water attacks. She'd let him drive because he knew where he was going.

And now she was glad he was driving, because there were a lot of people on these unfamiliar streets.

"Probably shouldn't mention the divorce papers," he answered without taking his eyes off the road.

"So I should be inappropriate instead, so she'll be glad to get rid of me?"

"Do you think the woman you just met would be turned off by inappropriate behavior?"

"Not really. She reminds me of my grandmother."

"Say that. Definitely say that."

Tarra laughed. "Not a chance."

His eyes drifted to her quickly before settling back on the road. "I did miss you," he said again.

Something caught in her chest.

Something warm and squishy and *completely* unwelcome.

The only thing more complicated than being dumped at the altar by the father of her baby was being still married to another guy who needed to *not* know she was pregnant.

Not her choice.

She wouldn't have hesitated to tell him.

Except being married to him while pregnant, even with another man's baby, meant that he, too, could sue for parental rights.

Did she think he would?

No.

But did she even know him?

Also no.

She would've sought the divorce with or without being pregnant.

So, on the advice of her attorney, she wasn't going to tell him. Given his mother's apparent grandmother fantasies, it was probably best anyway.

He pulled into the drive of an adorable yellow bungalow two blocks from the condo she'd rented. The street felt more like an alley, and he had to hop out and open a wide gate to pull onto the small concrete pad beside a flower garden that was already overgrown.

"To keep the tourists out," he said with a wry grin when he got back in the car and pulled it into the yard behind an old pickup truck.

He put his hand to her lower back and guided her to the front door. Which was completely unnecessary, because she could clearly see her way to the front door.

But she didn't mind the heat of his hand through her shirt.

It had been ten years since he'd touched her, but being close to him was easy. Whatever spark they'd had in Vegas was still there.

But they were both older, wiser, and still on different paths. Except this time, it seemed hers was the more serious, career-minded path of the two.

How had *that* happened?

"There's my Ben and his *wife*," Betty said as soon as they entered the cozy beach house that smelled like lasagna and fresh bread. "Whom his poor mother knew *nothing* about."

"I'm going to need to see the marriage license," a second voice announced.

One of the harem-women—the dark-haired one who'd been in the polka-dot bikini—stepped into the pastel living room with a glass of wine in hand.

Ben went stiff as a board. "Mom—"

"Don't you *mom* me." Betty wagged a finger. "We didn't get to see the wedding. You didn't have a reception. So I made sure to invite some friends over for your wedding dinner. So we can hear all about how you couldn't tell *your own mother* that you were getting married."

"Elvis swore we were just doing it for a promotional video," Tarra said. The truth? No. But close enough. She'd grown up one of thirteen kids. *Close enough* was practically her middle name. "That's the problem with Vegas. They give you a few drinks, ask you to sign a release and some other paperwork, and the next thing you know, you're getting official notification in the mail that you're married for real."

Ben slid her an unreadable look.

It might've been *thank you*.

Or it might've been *shut up now before you make this any worse*.

Always hard to tell when she hadn't seen or talked to her husband in a decade.

"It was a *Vegas* wedding?" Betty gasped.

"Oh, I did that once," a second woman said as she, too, joined them. She was the middle of the three women, with brown hair and brilliant blue eyes and a swishy beach dress covered with a short lime green cardigan. "Real estate convention. Two years ago. The divorce was totally painless. I can get you the guy's number."

Easy to read *that* look from Ben. Clearly he was wondering if she'd used the same attorney he and Tarra had used.

She shook her head. "He was arrested seven years ago," she whispered. "Apparently ours fell through the cracks when they were notifying victims whose paperwork hadn't been filed."

"When was this wedding?" the platinum blonde who'd also stepped into the living room wanted to know.

"Few years ago," Ben answered.

"A few *years* ago?" Betty dropped into a blue-and-white striped easy chair in front of a big potted palm. "My only son has been married for a few *years* and I'm just now finding this out?"

If Ben got any stiffer, he'd turn to stone. Tarra slipped an arm around his waist and squeezed. The man was solid. And he smelled like salt water and lime. And she kinda hoped he didn't put a shirt on for dinner.

Where *was* his shirt?

"It's complicated," she said to Betty.

"I'm sure we can uncomplicate it quickly," the dark-haired woman said.

Ben sighed, and his body seemed to sag. "Tarra, this is Emmanuelle, Chloe, and Nikita. My mother's friends."

Tarra smiled at the three of them. "Nice to meet you all."

"We're *your* friends too, Benji," Emmanuelle said.

She was clearly the dangerous one of the bunch. Poised, determined, and almost visibly calculating how much money she'd have to pay her Great Uncle Guido to have Tarra knocked off if she didn't get the hint and get out of the way.

Were there mob cells in little beach towns on this part of the Florida Gulf Coast?

Tarra didn't know.

Maybe she should've brought one of her sisters.

Or all ten of them.

She would've thought it was weird that Ben's mother had invited his harem, except her family probably would've done the same.

If any of her sisters had harems, that is. Her oldest brother was a priest, and her other brother swore his wife was lucky he'd given her the time of day after growing up with eleven sisters.

"Any friend of Ben's is a friend of mine too," Tarra said happily. "Are you all from Coconut Bay originally?"

They ignored her. Again.

This was going to be a fun dinner.

"Bennie, we're still on for the beach clean-up tomorrow morning, right?" Nikita said.

"I have the trash bags," Chloe added.

"I have maps," Emmanuelle announced.

"I have two feet and two hands," Tarra said.

"Wine?" Ben asked her.

"Hot water? I brought tea."

One eye crinkled at her. "More?"

"It's a lifestyle." And her livelihood.

A timer dinged, and Betty pulled herself out of the chair and headed to the kitchen. "My only son. A Vegas wedding."

"Need help with anything?" Tarra asked.

"I already got the salad," Chloe said.

"I set the table," Nikita added.

Emmanuelle looked Tarra up and down with a sniff. "I supervised."

"Undoubtedly." Tarra smiled.

Emmanuelle didn't.

"Do you drink tea?" Tarra asked her. "I have a few varieties specifically blended for stress relief." She reached into her purse and pulled out the travel bin. "Passion flower is my favorite, but if you like mint, you should try the peppermint lemon balm. It's delicious."

"I'll stick with my sangria," Emmanuelle said dryly.

As though she needed the alcohol to cope with Tarra.

Tarra sucked in a smile. She'd gotten over high school twenty years ago, and their attempts to take her back were lame, at best.

Life was too short to be bitchy. It was also too short to let bitchiness get her down.

"He married a hippie," Chloe whispered.

"It won't last," Nikita whispered back.

Ben sighed again. She could almost smell the tension radiating off him. Dinner was clearly not her best idea.

"Do you know how long it takes to brew a good Chinese tea?" Tarra asked him.

"I have no idea."

"An oolong time."

His dark eyes met hers, her heart stammered and lost its breath, and that was before his lips quirked up.

"I actually did some research last year into the tea they serve at Kensington Palace," she said. "Know what the most popular kind is?"

He shook his head.

"Royal tea."

He barked out a short laugh. "That was really bad."

She grinned. "I know. And I have a lot more. Know what you need before dinner?"

He was smiling so broadly now, his dimple had popped. How had she forgotten how cute he was? "I don't want to know, do I?"

"A tea-shirt."

"This is going to be the longest dinner ever," Nikita murmured.

Emmanuelle drained her sangria and went back to the kitchen.

Ben grabbed Tarra's hand. "You're probably right about the shirt." He tugged her down a short hallway to a small bedroom with a double bed, where he opened squeaky accordion doors on a closet and pulled out a faded gray Stanford T-shirt and slipped it over his head.

"You keep clothes at your mother's place?"

He winced, and the lingering smile disappeared. "I...live here."

"Oh."

"And we could both fit through the window so we don't have to suffer through dinner with..." he trailed off.

"The harem?" she suggested.

"They're *not* my harem."

"But it's really cute how your eyeball twitches every time I call them that."

His eye twitched again.

She smiled and reached up to smooth his brow. The minute her fingers made contact with his face, he sucked in a breath.

His gaze collided with hers, and she sucked in a breath too.

This was a trick of the hormones, she told herself. A normal reaction to an old flame. Basic chemistry. Or biology. Or something.

She didn't have time for a fling. Not with *anyone*, especially a man she needed to get a divorce from.

Whom she barely knew at all.

But whom her body remembered like their time together had been yesterday.

His hands settled at her waist, and she instinctively tried to suck her belly in, which didn't work so well. But thankfully, he didn't seem to notice.

"How do you do that?" he murmured.

"D-do what?" she stammered.

"I haven't seen you in ten years, but you touch me, and I want to kiss you again."

"That's just because I'm not someone your mother picked out."

"I don't think so."

And there went her heart stammering out a protest to her protests. Because he was so close, *so* close, and she could see the hints of gray mixed in with his dark stubble, the stress lines at the corners of his eyes that she wanted to smooth away, the matching creases starting in his forehead.

She wanted to know where he'd been the last decade. What he'd done. Why he was here. If he'd been back to Vegas.

If he meant it when he said he'd missed her.

She wanted to kiss him too.

"We can't do this," she whispered.

"Why not? We *are* married."

"But not for long."

"What if Vegas wasn't a mistake, Tarra? What if the divorce was a mistake?"

What if?

She shook her head and pushed at his chest. "Don't try that charm on me. I'm here as a favor to someone I have very fond memories of. I'm not here to be a pawn in your mother's game to find you a wife. A *real* wife. Not me."

He didn't move, so she pushed again, and this time, he let his hands drop. "Right. You have a life." He gestured to the door, this time without touching her. "After you."

She almost didn't go. Because there was something defeated, something almost *broken* in the way he wouldn't look at her.

As though her reminder of who they were—and weren't—to each other sliced deeper than she understood.

She swallowed her questions and headed for the voices in the kitchen.

If he'd honestly missed her, he'd had ten years to come find her.

She'd been a man's convenient bride once already this year. She wasn't falling into that trap again.

And she wanted to believe she'd stay strong even if she didn't have the baby growing inside her, but the fact that she couldn't say for sure meant she needed to get through this dinner and put some distance between herself and Ben.

Maybe her attorney was right.

Maybe she should've just mailed him the paperwork.

$\mathcal{B}$en had thought he'd been through hell before. There was losing his dad eight years ago. The call that his mom had been diagnosed with cancer sixteen months ago. Making the choice to walk away from his business, because—just *because*. He didn't want to talk about it.

He *never* wanted to talk about it.

But tonight, his new hell was dinner with his surprise wife, his mother, and his harem—dammit—his mother's three top picks for the next Mrs. Garcia.

Women were vicious.

Except Tarra.

Every time Nikita, Chloe, or Emmanuelle would take a subtle dig —*I helped Ben when he got stung by that jellyfish his first weekend here* with the *and where were you?* silently added to the end—Tarra would smile, say a sweet *that was so nice of you*, and tell a corny tea joke.

"What's with you and tea?" Chloe asked mid-dinner. "That's a really old-fashioned obsession."

"Actually, my average customer is about twenty-nine," Tarra

answered. "Specialty teas are exploding in popularity right now, especially with the younger generation."

"You work at a tea shop?" Emmanuelle demanded.

"I own a specialty online company called Naughtea."

Ben shoveled another bite of lasagna into his mouth to keep from gaping like the other women were.

Tarra was in business too. For herself. He could—no. *No.*

He couldn't give her any pointers. He wasn't a businessman. He was a beach bum.

"*Naughtea?*" his mom said. "Like...naughty dirty tea?"

"I started with aphrodisiac teas, because sex sells pretty much anything, and it's been so successful I've expanded into other varieties of health and wellness teas. And some are just for fun. We launched a line of mythological teas with unicorn tea, fairy tea, mermaid tea, and dragon tea about a month ago, and we can't keep it in stock."

"We?" Emmanuelle prompted.

"My staff and I. There are four of us."

Emmanuelle sniffed. "Well, I hope you're not looking for Ben to fund your little project. He doesn't do business anymore."

"Not since his business partner dropped dead of a heart attack at thirty-nine," Chloe added.

Tarra blinked and turned to look at him.

Questions. Shock. Pity.

Dammit.

His lasagna lodged somewhere behind his heart, his face went hot, and he clenched his fists so tight he bent the fork in his right hand.

"Dessert!" his mother said brightly. "We should have dessert. I have one of those frozen ice cream cakes that Ben loves so much. Tarra, do you eat ice cream? You look like one of those women who'd get a food baby for a week if you ate more than three pieces of lettuce. Not that there's anything wrong with that. Have you had your hormone levels tested? I hear beanpoles can sometimes have trouble conceiving, and you look like you might be pushing forty—"

Ben shoved to his feet. "Thanks for dinner, Mom. I'm taking Tarra home."

"Sweetheart, you *are* home."

"To *her* home."

"She's moving here?"

Tarra wiped her lips with the yellow-and-green checkered napkin, set it across her half-finished plate, and rose too. "Thank you so much for dinner, Betty. It was lovely meeting you. Chloe, Nikita, Emmanuelle, hope to see you again soon."

Chloe pulled a card out of her cleavage. "Call me if you're in the market for something permanent."

Emmanuelle poked her.

"What?" she hissed. "You wouldn't turn down a sale either."

"That won't be necessary," Tarra said dryly, waving away the card.

Which was the first non-upbeat thing she'd said since they left his bedroom.

His harem—as Tarra called them—all perked up.

But his mother frowned. "And will I see you again soon?"

"Thank you again for dinner," Tarra said.

She smiled, waved, and when she turned, he led her out of the house.

He shouldn't have agreed to bring her in the first place.

But just the sight of her had given him something he'd been short on the last fifteen months or so.

Hope.

But it didn't matter, because she was leaving. In two days. On Sunday.

And she'd go on with her life, with her business, with her family, with everything that gave her that innate happiness, and he'd be here.

With his mother trying to set him up with a harem.

While he tried to figure out what to do about this aimless feeling that had been gnawing at him for weeks.

Dusk was settling outside. Tarra didn't go to the passenger side of the car.

No, she walked around to the driver's side. "Thanks for dinner," she said lightly. "I don't mind eating by myself, but it's always nice to have company."

"You like eating with barracudas?"

She laughed, and he had to stop himself from grabbing her around the waist and trying to soak up some of that joy.

He'd shed the stress when he left California, but he still hadn't found his joy.

Not like she obviously had.

But then, she'd always had it.

"You can do better, Ben," she said softly.

He already had.

She held out her hand. "Keys, please?"

"I can drive you. No trouble."

"I think I should go back alone."

"You know what my mother's going to say to that?" It was weak, and made him look desperate, but he didn't care.

He didn't want to let her go.

"Tell your mother the truth. *All* of the truth."

Right. The part where Tarra was only here to deliver divorce paperwork that didn't get done ten years ago, and the part where he wasn't *ever* marrying Nikita, Chloe, or Emmanuelle.

Especially Emmanuelle.

"You're not leaving because I live with my mother, are you?" he tried to joke.

She smiled, a gentle bit of happiness lit by the rising moon. "It was good to see you again, Ben. I don't know what brought you here, but I hope you find where you fit."

He didn't make her ask again for the keys, but he did let his fingers linger against hers when he handed them over. "Took you ten years to want to get married again?"

She blinked and looked away. "Something like that."

"Can I at least get your phone number before you go?"

She hesitated.

"I'll sign the papers," he said. "But you—you've always been a bright memory. I missed you. Nothing says we can't get to know each other again, is there?"

This time, she studied him closer. It was too dark to see the green in her irises, but he could feel the scrutiny in her gaze.

As though she was deciding if he was worth the trouble.

He wasn't.

But he had no intention of telling her that.

"I'll text you," she finally said.

It took him a minute to catch up. "Because you already have my number."

"I do."

I do. He snorted to himself.

She pulled her hand away, went up on tiptoe, and kissed his cheek. "Thank you," she said.

She didn't elaborate on what for—for giving her the keys, in advance for opening the gate, for the torturous dinner, for agreeing to sign the papers—and he didn't ask.

But when her car turned the corner, long after he'd closed the gate up after her, he wished he'd gotten something more than just a *thank you* from her.

6

_____

*T*arra was up with the sun.

Not because she *wanted* to be, but because she had trouble sleeping.

She kept remembering that haunted look in Ben's face, the way his entire body seemed to freeze, when one of his mother's minions had mentioned his business partner.

It wasn't her business.

But no amount of telling herself that could erase the memory of the panic coupled with the pain that had crossed his features for that suspended moment before he shoved back from the table.

And no amount of knowing that she needed him to sign their divorce papers—they'd thought they were divorced for the last *ten years*—could erase the feeling of his hands wrapped around hers last night.

He'd gotten under her skin ten years ago. She'd thought she'd be more immune now, more mature, more confident, more *something*, but really, most of what she was, was sad.

Sad for Ben. Sad that they were over. Sad that she knew she wouldn't ever get to know him, because once they were divorced and he knew she had a baby on the way—if he ever called her, that was—

they'd undoubtedly drift back to being people who had fond memories of each other but never spoke.

She pulled on a loose cotton dress, fixed herself a cup of ginger tea —it had helped with morning sickness in her first trimester, and now it was habit—and poured it into a to-go mug before locking the condo behind her and heading the block to the beach. Even though the sun would rise over the land behind her, she still wanted to see the beach in the morning.

To walk with the seagulls.

See if there were any dolphins out playing this early in the day.

Get her feet wet in the gulf.

Snap a few pictures to send to her sisters. She'd group-texted with them for an hour or so after she got back to the condo last night. The usual questions—how had he taken the news, was he signing the papers, did any of Tarra's sisters need to come down here and kick his ass, and was she going to try to score one last time for old time's sake, or had he not aged well enough for that?

He'd aged well.

He'd aged exceptionally well.

But if she came with baggage, he came with a whole semitruck. And she felt for him—she did—but she couldn't solve his problems for him.

She'd tried that various times over the years for various men, and it never worked.

The beach was mostly deserted. Fluffy clouds, tinged pink and orange, drifted lazily over the deep blue water. So calm. So peaceful.

A flock of seagulls was gathered around a wet patch of sand littered with seaweed and small shells. She gave the birds a wide berth, stopping occasionally to snap pictures on her phone. A wooden pier extended into the gulf a block or so down, so she headed toward it, sipping her tea and swinging her sandals while her toes sank into the sand.

She was almost there when a flurry of white feathers suddenly whirled around her. Something thwacked her ear. Something else scratched her arm, and a third something—seagulls, all those *some-things*—pecked at her hair.

She flung her arms out, sending her tea and sandals flying, and then covered her head. "*Aaaahh!*"

Escape. Run. Duck.

No, not ducks. Seagulls.

She didn't pay attention to direction, she just ran. Something wet and goopy landed on her arm. Then more wet and goopy.

Feathers.

Claws.

Squawks.

And a man's voice. "Shoo, you dirty birds!"

The seagulls took flight, dozens of them sailing out over the water. Tarra's heart was in her throat, her pulse racing, her arms scratched and stinging.

And covered in bird poop.

That could *not* be good for the baby.

She flinched, moved her hands to wipe off the bird poop, then stopped.

She couldn't touch the bird poop. But it was already touching her.

And then she saw why the birds had left, and she stopped harder.

Ben.

Jogging toward her, waving his arms at the seagulls that hadn't cleared out to the water yet.

No, not jogging.

Running.

"Hey, whoa, you okay?" He stopped at her side, pulled off his T-shirt, revealing all that tone, bronze muscle, and went to work wiping her clean.

"They—they—"

"They're fucking insane," he said. "Jesus. You're bleeding. Come on. Let's get you cleaned up."

"My tea!"

She was such a dork. A goober. A mess.

Who cared about her tea?

His dark curls lifted, his brown eyes hit hers, and a distantly familiar, dimpled, warm smile lit his face. "Can't forget the tea."

She gave him a light shove. "Don't mock me."

"You got it, feathers."

"Feathers?"

He glanced down at her body. "If the bird part fi—holy shit, Tarra."

She looked down too.

The wind had flattened her dress against her abdomen, and apparently she'd popped overnight.

She twisted away. "Food baby," she lied.

"Tarra."

"I need to go get cleaned up." She walked—quickly—to where her tea mug had landed upside down in the sand, leaking all her ginger tea on the beach.

Ben jogged to keep up. "You're not still with him."

"This is none of your business, just like why you're here in Florida isn't any of my business."

"Is it his?"

The blood in her veins frosted over. She drew up short, turned, fisted her hand, and socked him in the arm at the implication that she'd be pregnant with anyone else's baby. "Sign the damn papers and leave me alone."

She didn't add *asshole*.

She didn't have to.

It was clearly understood.

7

*S*aturdays were usually busy days on the beach. Over the winter, Ben had inherited the full-time job of setting up beach umbrellas from Palm Street over to Bay Avenue, charging the tourists twenty bucks a pop to use his shade.

Most of the money went back into the Coconut Bay coffers, because he didn't need the money, and running the umbrellas meant he got to sit on the beach all day long.

Today, he slipped the neighbor's college kid a fifty and told him to keep anything over the normal five hundred bucks for watching the chairs today.

Then he hit the shops.

He hated shopping.

Especially on Palm Street, because all the locals knew he had cash.

But it was necessary today.

Two hours after he'd uttered the stupidest words known to man, he was back at Tarra's door, hoping she'd let him in.

After the sixth time he knocked, she opened it with a glare. "What?"

"I didn't mean that how it sounded." Before she could slam the door in his face, he shoved the two overstuffed brown bags at her. "Peace offering. I'm sorry."

She peeked down.

Her eyes narrowed.

Because she was mad that he'd clearly taken the easy way out? Or because she was mad that it was the generic grocery store variety of tea instead of something named after unicorns or sexual positions?

Yeah, he'd looked up Naughtea last night.

Might've ordered some Doggie Style Tea too.

Not that he was confessing.

"You realize there's no way for that to sound *right*."

This was good. She was talking. Not slamming the door in his face. "I just don't understand why a guy would walk away from you." Especially in her condition.

"You walked away too," she reminded him.

Ouch.

Yeah, that hit its mark. Bulls-eye right to the chest.

He glanced down at her belly, once again covered in ruffles. "I wouldn't have, if..."

"Did you bring the paperwork?"

Right. She didn't need any man supporting her.

Or her baby.

Just—holy *shit*.

Tarra was having a baby. "Oh, hell—some of that tea has caffeine in it. Can you—I didn't think—I'll take it back. Sorry. But the dolphin statue is completely caffeine-free. Cross my heart. So's the dart gun for shooting at the stuffed seagull."

She sighed, a smile finally teasing at the corners of her mouth, and he drew a full breath for the first time since he'd seen her in the middle of that flock of seagulls.

Those birds could be scary as hell, and he couldn't deny that his heart had stopped once or twice while he sprinted across the beach to reach her.

And that was before he'd realized *her* well-being wasn't the only one at stake.

"You're not leaving, are you?" she asked.

"I don't want to, but I will if you want me to."

She stepped back and opened the door wider. "Come on in then."

Women were so confusing. He offered to leave, and she let him stay.

Or maybe they weren't so confusing after all.

He carried the bags through the entryway, past the bedroom door and the living room, and into the kitchen. Once he had them on the counter, he reached inside for the paperwork he'd signed this morning.

Even though every stroke of the pen had felt wrong.

She wasn't his. She never had been.

And he was an asshole for suggesting they stay married. In ten years, he hadn't once sought her out or tried to find her. He'd been too busy in California.

Or maybe he'd been too afraid of what he'd find.

That she'd moved on without him. That she didn't remember him. That their time together had been *normal* for her, while it had shifted something inside him he hadn't wanted or been able to acknowledge for a long time.

For ten years, if he was being honest with himself.

She watched him carefully while he handed over the paperwork. All of it neat and tidy in a black folder.

The formal dissolution of three days of magic in Vegas ten years ago.

She was still watching him when she took the folder, still studying his face, as though she were looking for something.

For what, he couldn't tell. He couldn't read her expression.

Disappointment? Relief? Anger? Suspicion?

She glanced down and flipped through the packet. "You didn't want to have your own attorney look this over?"

He shook his head. "I read it."

Was he brilliant in legalese? No. But they'd never combined assets, bought anything together bigger than a meal and ten minutes with Elvis, and they didn't have any children.

He might not have googled Tarra *before* she showed up at the parade yesterday, but that didn't mean he hadn't spent a few hours digitally stalking her last night.

And he was certain this was her first baby.

"Thank you," she said softly.

Her hand settled on her lower belly, and an emotion he couldn't name clogged his entire chest.

He could name the ugly slither crawling up his spine though.

That was easy.

Regret.

Ten years ago, he'd gotten cold feet. Freaked out over the idea of introducing free-spirited, fun-loving Tarra into his cutthroat corporate world. Worried over what the board would've said about his Vegas wedding. Panicked that he'd ruined the career he'd worked so long to build by uttering two little words to a ray of sunshine in a gaudy chapel on the Strip.

How different would his life have been if he'd said screw the career, screw the judgment, screw the gossip, instead of letting her go?

He cleared his throat. "Ever been on a dolphin cruise?"

She blinked. "Are you asking because you know a guy, or because you want me to go on one with you?"

"Both."

She didn't answer right away.

"Just because we're divorced doesn't mean we can't be friends," he added with what he hoped was an easy smile.

Friends.

He wasn't sure he knew how to be *friends*.

But he knew he had one more day to spend with the happiest, brightest, most fun woman he'd ever met.

"Will there be seagulls on the boat?" she asked with a wry grin.

His smile was suddenly easier than it had been in months. "If there are, I'll take care of them for you."

"You know I can usually take care of anything I need myself."

"I have no doubt. But it would be a huge boost to my ego if you let me play the dashing hero for an afternoon."

Her phone dinged three times in rapid succession. She glanced at it, laughed, and then smiled up at him. "Okay. A dolphin tour sounds great. Thank you."

"You came all the way here. It's the least I can do."

The very, very least.

8

*T*he weight Tarra had expected to lift once she had the signed divorce papers was still there. Some of the stress was gone, but there was something else in its place.

Something that felt like dangerous affection.

She was pregnant with another man's baby. She didn't need to be getting all goopy-eyed over a guy who was acting like he'd suddenly just realized what he'd lost.

She tucked the signed papers into her suitcase in the bedroom, then breezed back to the kitchen. He was head-down over his phone, setting up the dolphin cruise.

"Hungry? Thirsty?" she asked him.

His dark gaze lifted, that thick ring of lashes accentuating his attention. His eyes lingered on her lips just long enough to make them tingle before he shook his head and looked back down at his phone. "All set for eleven with Captain Jojo. Your phone keeps dinging."

It dinged twice, as though to punctuate his observation. "My sisters." She scanned the messages. "They want pictures of me with a dolphin."

"Got a statue down Palm Avenue a ways."

"You do? I missed that yesterday. Let's go." She tossed a few granola bars and bottles of water in her tote bag, then paused. "Are we going to get wet?"

He grinned. "Not today. Unless we toss you off the dolphin boat, but Captain Jojo says that's bad for repeat business, so she's only let me do it once."

She laughed. "You did not." She couldn't picture Ben tossing anyone. He'd been fun in Vegas, but also very by-the-rules. She'd had to work hard to talk him into skinny dipping in the hotel's pool, and she'd never forgot the utter shock on his face when she'd suggested the Bellagio's fountain first.

His smile slid into a frown. "True enough."

He snagged her bag and carried it down the concrete stairs on the exterior of the condo building. "Don't suppose you'd hold my hand in public to spark some rumors," he murmured softly.

"Is this a ploy to touch me, or a ploy to get your mother off your back?"

"Both."

"You didn't sign those papers with disappearing ink, did you?"

He barked out a laugh. "No. You're free."

"Hm."

They hit the bottom step, turned up Lemongrass Way, and headed for Palm Avenue. And Tarra slipped her hand into his.

His fingers tightened briefly, warm and snug, before relaxing into a loose hold. "There's a fountain up a little farther," he told her. "You'd buy me an extra two weeks if you kissed me there."

"Hand-holding is free, but you have to earn the kisses."

"I saved you from a rabid flock of seagulls."

"And I saved you from your mother's harem."

He shuddered.

"Which one do you think you'll pick?" she asked.

The abject horror that creased his features made her laugh again.

"None," he said very distinctly.

"Then you should tell them that."

"I'd have to move back across the country to avoid the fallout."

"Is that why you came here in the first place? You had another harem that got out of hand?"

He squeezed her hand again. "Very smooth. Slipped that in there when I wasn't looking."

"But you're not answering."

Why he was here wasn't her business. She knew that. But she still couldn't help prodding him. "You know what I remember about you?"

"My killer dance moves?"

"Your suit."

He grimaced.

She bumped his shoulder as they walked. "It fit you."

"It was custom-made."

"No, I mean you *being* in a suit fit your personality. I thought."

"It did," he acknowledged slowly.

She glanced at him and kept walking. The scent of frying bacon wafted out from Coconut Bay Diner, and a gentle breeze brought in a soft hint of salt water too. All the shops and restaurants on Palm Avenue were painted in pastels, except for the mega tourist stores and their glass fronts covered in painted advertisements for boogie boards and beach chairs and shark tooth necklaces. Hibiscus plants bloomed in planter boxes along the sidewalk, and the sun warmed her bare arms.

Her phone was buzzing regularly—her sisters could group text like champs, especially on a Saturday morning—but she ignored it and tilted her face up to the sky while she waited for Ben to fill in any gaps he felt necessary.

He didn't owe her any explanations. They were friends. Or something. And they'd probably never talk again after this weekend. But she was nosy. And she got the sense he was as unsettled now as she'd been ten years ago when they got married.

When she'd looked at him—a successful businessman, barely older than she was, who knew what he was supposed to do with his life and had been *doing* it, with no fear—she'd realized she didn't want to be a corporate monkey filing paperwork.

The day she'd gotten home from Vegas had been the day she developed her business plan.

Tea isn't popular, she'd been told over and over.

Tea is an old person's drink, the banks had said. *Your customer base will just die, and they're too old for aphrodisiacs anyway*.

But then a certain risqué book had exploded and been covered by every news channel, Millennials had come of age looking to be *different*, and suddenly *everyone* wanted aphrodisiacs *and* unique teas.

So here she was.

Living her dream.

While he was living someone's dream, but she wasn't sure if it was his.

"Money's not much good if you're dead," he finally said. "Lucas—my partner—and I were in mergers and acquisitions. Working twenty hours a day. Hooked up to coffee IVs. Sometimes we were the good guys, sometimes we were the bad guys. The stress—it was an addiction. A badge of honor. *I only got six hours of sleep last week but I made three million dollars*. That sort of bullshit."

"So, no yoga classes or aromatherapy time?" she asked.

He snorted. "No. No yoga or hippie therapy. Just work, coffee, vodka, and hypertension. We'd just closed on the biggest deal of our career when Lucas keeled over in his chair in the boardroom. He was thirty-nine. Left behind a wife and a baby. She spit in my face at his funeral, and I can't say I blame her. We pushed each other too hard, and left everything—everyone—else behind."

"So you walked away," she finished softly.

"Flew out here for perspective. Two days later Mom was diagnosed with colon cancer."

She squeezed his hand, because there wasn't anything she could say that would make his losses and grief any easier.

"She's good now," he added, and a wry smile lightened his face. "But getting sick made her very determined to be a grandmother sooner rather than later."

"How long was she in treatment?"

"Just over a year. Had her colostomy reversal surgery six weeks ago. She's pretty much back to normal. What counts as normal, anyway."

"So what's next for you?"

"A lazy life on the beach."

But the corners of his eyes tightened, and his voice held a hint of strain.

"So you'll be a beach bum forever then?" she teased lightly.

"Appears so. Ah, here we are. A dolphin, just for you."

She had a feeling there was more to Ben than just wanting to bum around a beach town, but she dropped it. She was being too nosy again. Plus, he'd found her a dolphin, as promised.

The main intersection in town had a giant fountain right in the center of the road. A brick sidewalk circled it, with dolphin statues standing guard at the four corners.

He took her phone and snapped a few pictures for her, and he was about to hand it back when his eyes went comically wide. "Okay, then."

She grabbed the phone, and—of course.

Cinna, her baby sister, had texted a request for a naked picture of Ben. Which he had undoubtedly seen.

He was grinning again, which was a relief. "You've been talking to your sisters about me."

"No, that's the other Ben I married and didn't divorce either after you."

"You know your nose turns pink when you're lying?"

"That wasn't a lie. It was sarcasm. Oh, wow. Is that saltwater taffy? The kind they pull right in the shop? I haven't had that in *years*." She glanced both directions, then crossed the deserted street and made a beeline for the corner candy store, because she was *not* discussing *anything* else that her sisters had said or speculated about him.

He opened the door and steered her inside. "You have dinner plans? I could fix you a six-course saltwater taffy dinner."

She laughed. "No, thank you. I've had enough puking the last three months for an entire lifetime. But I should take some souvenirs back for my nieces. Oh! And I have a nephew now. Two nephews. Can you believe it? We never thought there'd be anything but girls in the family."

"You know what you're having?" he asked while she perused the barrels of different taffy flavors.

"Nope. I want to be surprised."

She caught him smiling at her.

"What?"

"I just—that's exactly what I thought you'd say." He pulled his hands out of his pockets and picked up a box from the wooden shelf on the wall. "Chocolate dolphin?"

"My sisters would hate me and my nieces and nephews would adore me."

"How many?"

She frowned. "I haven't counted them lately. Just grab two dozen. Oh! Are those chocolate turtles? I need a couple dozen of those too."

"You want to just buy the whole store?"

She laughed and gave him a playful shove. "Hush up. You wanted to be my hero. Right now, that means helping me carry a few tons of chocolate and candy back to my condo."

"Juanita can ship it for you."

She clapped. "Oh, that's brilliant."

He grinned and shook his head again.

"What?"

"You're excited over postage. That's…"

"Insane? Weird? Very *carpe diem* of me?"

"I was going to say adorable."

She winked at him. "That part was understood."

He laughed and waved to a woman who'd just entered from another part of the candy store. "Morning, Juanita. We're going to need some boxes."

9

Since Tarra refused to let him buy candy for her nieces and nephews, Ben insisted on paying for the dolphin tour.

Not that he had ever intended to give her a choice. He'd already worked out payment with Captain Jojo.

"Wait. Where's everyone else?" Tarra asked as they stepped onto the sailboat.

"Private tour," Captain Jojo replied. She was a crusty lady a few years older than his mom, with a weathered face, wispy white hair, and a grip of steel. "Welcome aboard. Always glad to have honey-mooners."

"We're not—" Tarra started as Ben choked on air.

Captain Jojo laughed. "That's not what Betty Garcia told me. Don't go getting on her bad side now. Took that Nikita girl four months of delivering tuna casseroles every week before she got to join the approved list. Don't know what you did last night, but you just moved to the top of the list."

"It's because we're already married," Ben supplied.

When Tarra shot him a warning look, he shook his head. *I'll straighten them out later. Hush and enjoy the dolphin ride.*

Her eyes narrowed, but only for a moment before her mouth

spread in a wide smile. "I always did like being on top," she said cheerfully.

Damn, now he was picturing her naked, in a hotel room in Vegas, riding him and gasping in pleasure while he teased her breasts and found that magic button between her legs.

He swallowed hard.

"I think it's more than that," Jojo said while she tied off the ropes and shoved the sailboat from the dock. "You mud wrestle Emmanuelle or something?"

"She was nice," Ben supplied.

"Oh. In that crowd, being nice will do it."

His mom hadn't voiced her approval to him—she'd probably been afraid she'd jinx something if she did. But who could object to Tarra?

She was easy to talk to, she was successful in her own business, and she could hold her own without stooping to insults and pettiness.

If she was sticking around—

He squelched that thought before it could fully form. Because she *wasn't* sticking around, and he wasn't in a position to be anybody's partner right now.

She deserved something more than a guy who'd asked her to stay married just so he didn't have to tell his mother he wasn't planning on settling down.

Ever.

Because what happened when the guilt of doing nothing with his life got to be too overwhelming, and he went back to work, and once again found that high in business?

What happened when he missed too many dinners? When he didn't know his own kids? When he drove himself to an early grave?

His mom was better now. He could move out. Get his own place.

And still be a lazy beach bum.

He was a fucking awesome lazy beach bum.

Or at least awesome enough that he could play one on TV.

A hand settled on his knee. He glanced up and found Tarra watching him curiously. "You okay?"

"Yep." He held out his other hand. "Here. Give me your phone. I'll get a picture of you on the boat."

Instead of handing it over, she scooted closer to him, pulled it out, and held it up in front of them. She was in a floppy straw hat—though not as big as Chloe's had been yesterday—and sunglasses with glittery pink rims, with an orange life vest covering the puffy blouse that hid her baby bump.

"Smile," she said. "No! Wait. Make duck lips. My sister Margie *hates* when people make duck lips."

She snapped several selfies while Captain Jojo expertly steered the sailboat out of the harbor and toward the normal dolphin hangouts in the gulf. Before they lost signal, she shot two of the best off to her group text with her sisters.

"They're going to think something's going on," he told her.

She grinned. "I know. I love messing with their heads. Oh! Look! What was that?"

"Dolphin pod," Captain Jojo called.

Tarra leaned over the side of the boat. *Way* far over.

Ben grabbed her by the strap on her life vest.

If she went over—

Hell, if she went over, he'd probably go in after her. And then he'd kiss her silly in the water, because—

No.

No kissing. No *because*.

She was leaving.

She came here for a divorce.

She was having another man's baby.

End of story.

She grinned up at him. "They're so close!"

He glanced down again, and two dolphins surfaced out of the clear blue water right beside the boat.

"Hansel and Gretel," Jojo told them. "Those two are always together. Dolphins mate for life, you know."

Hansel and Gretel rolled out of the water again beside them, and this time—

Tarra shrieked. "Was that—"

"Mating season," Jojo said. "Hansel's feeling frisky." She winked at Ben.

Like she expected he was feeling frisky too.

Tarra was laughing. She was *so* damn pretty when she laughed. So carefree. So full of life.

"Animal sex is funny?" Ben teased.

"My sister Sage is going to be very unhappy that she missed this."

"She's into animal sex?"

"She's a vet. She tortures us with stories of dogs and cats and guinea pigs humping every Thanksgiving and Easter."

"Haven't lived until you've seen octopi mating," Jojo called from the steering wheel. "Look up on the left—got a dozen or so dolphins coming up."

Ben followed Tarra to the other side of the sailboat and leaned into her on the seat, pointing at the next pod of dolphins surfacing. "There. See them?"

She leaned back against him, and his heart cranked up. "They're so gorgeous. I'd be out here watching them every day if I lived here."

"They blend in after a while."

She clamped a hand to her hat as a strong breeze caught them, and she looked back at him. "That's sad."

"Where do you live?"

"Right now? Next door to one sister, sharing a house with another, in this adorable little wedding-obsessed town southwest of Chicago."

He wasn't touching *wedding-obsessed*. "Lots of corn fields?" He didn't know that much about the Midwest.

"Lots of dirt fields right now."

"You pay attention to them every day?"

"I do. I keep waiting to see when the farmers are going to plow, and then plant, and then we get to watch the plants go from little green fuzz for miles all around, into little baby corn plants, and then tall corn stalks. And once it's tall and strong, I wonder how long it'll be before I get to eat all the corn. Have you ever had fresh corn on the cob? Right out of the field, grilled over a hot fire? It's delicious. Like corny heaven."

"Corny heaven?"

"Yep. And there are edamame fields too."

When his brow furrowed, she laughed. "Soybeans," she explained.

"Ah."

She straightened and leaned over the boat, watching for dolphins. Captain Jojo explained some of the history of Coconut Bay and this part of the Gulf Coast, exaggerating the pirate tales, pointing out the lighthouse north of town, dropping hints about the best—most expensive—seafood restaurants and where to find the most delicious hush puppies.

And all the while, Tarra marveled and squealed and exclaimed over the dolphins.

She was, in a word, *joy*.

In another word, she was addictive.

Ben was happier for just watching *her* happiness.

Happiness had been elusive the last ten years. He'd thought he was happy—with every success, ever takeover, every additional million dollars in his bank account, he'd smiled. He'd pumped his fist.

But every successive million made him less happy than the million before, and made him more eager to work harder and longer until he could get that same high that he'd gotten off his first major acquisition.

He hadn't found it.

He hadn't found it here, in Coconut Bay, either.

Not the town's fault. He'd been worried about his mother, and then there was the harem situation, but everyone else was friendly. The tourists didn't bother him. Couldn't ask for better weather, though they'd had a nasty hurricane scare last season, and he was sure they'd have another one or four this year too.

And the scenery and wildlife were beyond compare.

So why did it take this one woman less than twenty-four hours to finally make him see what he'd been missing?

Captain Jojo brought them back to the dock too soon. He stood and followed Tarra off the boat, slipping Jojo an extra fifty on his way off.

She took his cash and winked at him. "Keep that smile, Ben. Looks good on you."

His gaze trailed after Tarra, who had paused and was eyeing a lone seagull on a dock post, and his lips curved into a smile so big his cheeks hurt. "Wish it was that simple, Jojo," he murmured.

He truly did.

10

*T*arra bit into a fried shrimp over dinner at a cute little tiki bar on the water, and she couldn't stop the groan of pleasure that slipped out her lips. "This is the *best* seafood I've ever had."

Ben shifted across from her, looking momentarily pained before he smiled back. "You gonna need seconds?"

"No." She pursed her lips. "But I wouldn't turn them down."

He laughed. Since the dolphin sail, he'd taken her on a driving tour up the coast until they'd stopped and wandered through a nature preserve right on the beach where they'd ended up holding hands and telling stories about things they'd each done the last ten years.

Mostly she'd told the stories.

His all seemed to revolve around work, and he frowned every time he mentioned his old life. But with twelve total siblings, and the number of nieces and nephews seeming to grow by the day, she could've told four hours' worth of stories and not even made it from last Thanksgiving to Christmas.

She excused herself to use the bathroom—again—and when she returned to the table, Ben was ordering another plate of shrimp, and there was a new basket of hush puppies on the table.

"Thank you," she said to him as she slid back into her seat.

He smiled, more of another glimpse of the Ben she'd known ten years ago. "I like watching you eat."

She laughed. "I meant for everything today. This was fun. I didn't know what to expect when I got here yesterday, and..." She trailed off with a shrug. "I guess you could say I was ready for things to not be quite so easy."

He reached over the table and took her hand. "Do you have to leave tomorrow?"

Her heart leapt. And reality promptly put it back in its place. "I do." She didn't.

Not really.

She could run Naughtea from anywhere—since she sourced production of the tea to a small company in Maryland, most of her work was online.

But she knew what he was asking.

Stay, and see if this energy between them, this attraction, could go somewhere.

Commitment wasn't something she could give to a man right now.

She had her baby to concentrate on.

And she'd already married Ben spur of the moment once. She wasn't at all immune to his charms, and a guy who'd chase off seagulls, deliver every kind of tea he could find in the small local grocery store, and treat her to a fabulous day of playing tourist was her kind of charming.

He didn't push.

The second plate of shrimp came, and while she packed it away, he found few stories about deep sea fishing, or adventures in watching the tourists on the beach. But when he told her about streaking naked down Palm Avenue at midnight on Christmas Eve, she laughed so hard she almost choked on her shrimp.

"You did *not*," she said when she could talk again.

"Mom had gotten us an invitation to Emmanuelle's family's Christmas Eve party. They had a lot of good cocktails."

"And?"

"And I drank all of them."

She lifted her brows.

He grinned sheepishly. "And I was hoping that if I got arrested for public intoxication and nudity, that Emmanuelle's family would threaten to disown her if she didn't find herself a more suitable... whatever I am."

"Why don't you just tell them you're not interested? Or are you?"

She didn't want him to be interested.

Which wasn't fair, because he wasn't hers, but he was just *wrong* with those three women.

"I just...didn't care enough," he replied with a shrug.

Her heart dipped. This wasn't the man she remembered from Vegas at all. "Ben, are you okay?"

He sat straighter, his dark eyes coming to focus on her, as though the question startled him. Just when she thought he'd blink and look away, he replied. "I don't know what I want to be when I grow up," he said, almost as though the words were both a secret shame and a relief. He gave a rueful chuckle. "Crazy, right? Staring down forty, not sure what I want to be when I grow up."

"Life isn't a straight path. And I don't think any of us ever really grow up. The generation behind us just thinks we do."

He squeezed her hand. "You grew up."

"I just spent a day squealing over dolphins and lizards and buying enough candy to give an entire state a sugar buzz."

"That's grabbing life by the balls and holding on for the ride. But you—you're gonna be a mom."

"Which is both the most exciting and terrifying thing I've ever done, and I'll probably fake my way through half of it."

"You have a successful business."

"Which is way too much fun to be called a business. And if you tell the IRS that, I'll kill you."

He laughed, and she let herself relax.

But only a little.

"What did you want to be when you were little?" she asked.

"Han Solo."

"No way. I wanted to be Princess Leia."

He nodded. "I can see that. You, with the big braids around your ears and a bunch of furry creatures worshipping you…"

She realized mid-laugh that she'd never laughed this much with Jack.

How was that possible?

She'd been so dumb.

Ben lifted his brows.

"Just remembered I think I forgot to take my vitamin today," she said.

"Do you do that twitchy finger thing every time you lie?"

"I'm not lying. I did forget to take my vitamin today."

"But that's not what you were thinking about." He leaned closer. "Tarra Blue, do you have a secret?"

She had lots of secrets.

Most involved pranks she'd pulled on her siblings that other siblings had been blamed for, but when you were the fourth oldest of thirteen, you learned how to be a sneak.

"Maybe," she whispered, because flirting with a handsome guy on a wooden deck overlooking a gorgeous purple sunrise on the beach was pretty much heaven.

Especially when he was smiling back.

The guy she'd found sitting at the parade yesterday—the *water* parade—hadn't been smiling.

He'd been going through the motions.

Much like the man who'd sat next to her at that awkward as hell dinner party at his mother's house last night.

But this guy—he was *here*. In the moment. Smiling at her.

"What do I have to do to get your secrets?" he asked.

She wagged a finger at him. "Ex-husbands never get the best secrets."

He laughed.

And then she laughed.

Because this was ridiculous and weird but somehow, it was *right*.

"You're my favorite ex-husband," she informed him.

"I'm your only ex-husband." His eyes went wide. "Aren't I?"

"Technicalities."

"But I *am* your only ex-husband."

"Unless that weird dance around the fire with that guy in Tahiti was—"

He leaned over the table and silenced her with a kiss.

It was a soft kiss—at first—that surprised her enough into sucking in a breath, but there was something about his lips on hers that was so *right*, so familiar, so *everything* that it had been ten years ago, that when he moved to pull away, she fisted his T-shirt and pulled him closer, kissing him back, slow and thorough, until he hooked a hand behind her neck, his fingers tangled in her hair, his tongue gliding against hers, and she was suddenly ten years younger, at another sunset, blowing on a coin and teasing the handsome guy with the dress shirt rolled up his forearms. *I just cursed you. You're going to lose everything.*

And he'd hit the jackpot.

Except she'd felt like *she'd* won.

Because he'd turned around and kissed her.

Just like this.

He fit.

They fit.

Except she wasn't ten years younger. She wasn't looking for an escape from the boring normalcy of her life.

She needed to remember everything her life was now.

Even if all she wanted was to keep kissing him. To climb over the table, straddle him in that chair, and feel every inch of his body. To lose herself in the sensation of his touch, his taste, his sounds.

But she'd just gotten out of one relationship with a man who hadn't wanted all of her even before she got pregnant. She wasn't about to jump into another.

Even if she wanted to believe Ben *could* want all of her.

She reluctantly pulled back. "Wow," she whispered.

He brushed a thumb over her lower lip. His eyes were dark as night, his breath just as quick as hers. "Lightning," he said softly. "It's always lightning."

A streak flashed over the sky.

"Oh. Lightning."

He looked over his shoulder, back at the gathering storm clouds, and he shook his head. "No, Tarra, I meant—"

Thunder boomed, cutting him off.

"Well, aren't you two just cozy and cute?" Chloe—or was it Nikita? —stopped at the edge of their table. "Is that the fried Gulf shrimp? Aw, Bennie, remember when we shared that here two weeks ago?"

Nikita. She was the one who called him *Bennie*.

Which made his eye twitch, she noticed. "The shrimp's delicious," Tarra said. "Good choice. Did you get the hush puppies too? I think the strawberry butter just changed my entire life."

And now Nikita's eye was twitching. For a beach town, there was a lot of twitching going on.

"We heard the most awful rumor today," she said. "We heard y'all are getting *divorced*."

"Nikita—" Ben started.

Tarra lifted the plate between them. "Shrimp? We can't possibly eat all of this."

She didn't want to hear him say the words. *Yes, we're divorced.*

Did he need to tell them? Yes.

But for the first time since she'd found out she was still married to him, she didn't know how she felt about all the paperwork.

It had been a necessity two days ago.

Now, coming here felt like…something else.

Something she didn't want to name.

"No, thank you," Nikita said.

Tarra shrugged. "They really are delicious. Plus, there's that aphrodisiac power…"

"I've never heard that."

Probably because it wasn't true. "It didn't work for you when you two shared it?"

Ben coughed. He caught their server's eye and flipped out a credit card. "We need a to-go box."

"Where are y'all going?" Nikita asked.

"Somewhere my mother can't hear us," Ben answered.

Tarra shivered.

That sounded like a promise.

Except she knew that any further intimacy was a bad, bad idea. She was his excuse.

Not what he actually wanted.

*T*he air was fresher tonight. Or maybe it wasn't, but tonight, Ben noticed.

He sipped the pineapple tea Tarra had fixed him, and watched her while she sat with her knees tucked beneath her in the chair beside his on the condo's porch. She was telling another of her stories—this one about moving in with her sister, Pepper, after the wedding had fallen through, temporarily leaving her homeless. "Her dog is the most adorable creature in the entire universe. She hops like a bunny. I keep wondering what she'd do in the sand."

"Dig for carrots," he said.

She laughed.

He was rapidly becoming addicted to that sound.

"Have you ever had pets?" she asked.

He told her about Sparky, the golden retriever he'd had as a kid. One story led to another, the night insects chirped, the darkness deepened, and in the distance, another storm gathered over the water, occasionally illuminating the Gulf with brilliant white and yellow flashes. He realized she was stifling a yawn, and his tea was long gone.

He should go.

But he didn't want to.

That feeling he'd been looking for since he left California—*this* was it.

Peace.

Comfort.

Companionship.

Tarra had no expectations of him beyond him giving her back her freedom, which he'd done. In another life, in another time, they could've been friends.

No, they could've been more than friends.

She suddenly gasped and put a hand to her belly.

He straightened, knocking his cup over and banging a knee into the coffee table. His heart vaulted into a sprint, and terror coiled his gut. "Tarra? What's wrong?"

"I think the baby just kicked," she whispered.

It took him a second to process her answer.

In that second, she grabbed his hand and pulled it to her belly. She was so slender, his fingers covered her entire baby bump. "There. Did you feel it? It was just a flutter, like gas or something, but—*Ben*. My baby's kicking."

Her voice was a mix of wonder and waterworks.

He couldn't feel a thing—he didn't have the first clue what he was supposed to be feeling *for*, but he wanted to.

He wanted to sit on this porch, sipping tea, rubbing his hand over her belly every night until he *could* feel something.

She swiped her eyes and laughed softly. "Sorry. I'm not usually a crier. But—I haven't felt her kick before. I thought I was getting too old for babies, and now—now she's kicking me."

His own throat clogged.

He wasn't too old for babies. But in the years after Vegas, he'd gotten so wrapped up in work, watched Lucas get married after his girlfriend got pregnant, heard their arguments, and he'd tell himself after he made the next big score, he'd take a break and date a little.

That they'd slow down.

It hadn't happened.

And once he'd arrived in Coconut Bay, he'd felt so far removed from knowing who he was and what he wanted, he hadn't bothered seeking out women on his own.

There'd been the occasional tourist to scratch an itch or to escape the reality of his mom's illness every now and then, but nothing serious.

He'd just made peace with the idea of being on his own forever.

And then Tarra arrived.

With her own little miracle.

The one that he almost wished was his.

He was still palming her stomach. Her hand settled over his, holding him there, and the drum of his heart gradually shifted away from the panic, away from the regret, and took up a tune that was more like a *want*.

A wish.

A need.

He wished he hadn't panicked in Vegas.

That he'd gotten her number.

That he'd tracked her down, instead of waiting ten years for her to do it.

He'd been a fool.

"Tarra?"

"Hm?"

"This is the best day I've had in years."

She held his gaze in the moonlight, and that wish grew stronger. If he could bottle today and relive it every day for the rest of his life, he would.

She stroked a hand down his hair. "It's been spectacular."

This time tomorrow, she'd be back in Illinois. In fifteen hours or so, she'd be leaving to drive to the airport.

Fifteen hours wasn't enough time.

Fifteen days—hell, fifteen *years* wouldn't be enough time.

He'd missed his chance to get to know her better after Vegas. He wouldn't make the same mistake twice. "You ever see manatees?

There's a nature preserve an hour or so up the coast where we could find them. And I didn't get to take you up in the lighthouse yet. Or to the haunted cabin. And the snorkeling in the springs a little inland is unbelievable."

Her fingers drifted down his chest. "That's a lot to cover in a single morning."

"You could come back."

He held his breath while she studied him. So delicate, but so strong, so full of life. So optimistic.

"I don't think so," she whispered.

Which was the first negative thing Tarra had said all day.

His heart sank. "Why?"

"Because I don't trust myself to not get ideas."

"I like ideas."

"We barely know each other."

"I know enough to know I want to know more."

Her lips parted. He rushed on before she could offer another objection. "I'm not spontaneous. Getting married in Vegas? That wasn't like me. But meeting you—getting swept away, having the time of my life for those three days—those are the best memories of my life. The only thing I regret about that weekend was letting you go."

She pursed her lips.

No need to say what she was thinking. He knew.

But you did. You let me go.

"I was a ruthless son of a bitch in business, but a total chicken shit when it came to my heart," he confessed.

She rubbed his hand, still on her belly, then gently pulled it off and pressed it back on his own knee. "And it turns out I'm a ruthless mother-to-be," she said softly. "Ben, I will *always* treasure every memory I have of you, but I have some bigger priorities right now. And you have a few things to sort out. I've been a man's escape before. I can't do it again. Not when there's someone else who's going to need everything I have."

"Tarra—"

She rose and put a finger to his lips. "Thank you. For *everything*. For an amazingly fun day. For signing the papers and making all this easy. And for understanding that we can stay friends, but we can't be more."

"I don't understand."

"Yes, you do."

He did.

He got it.

He was an aimless shell of a man. And it wasn't her job to put him back together. She hadn't broken him. He'd done that to himself.

"I need to get my beauty rest," she said lightly as she pulled back and crossed past him to the sliding door leading into the small kitchen. "Thank you. Again. For everything."

He sat there, staring at the door, watching her slip out of sight.

And he had the overwhelming feeling he'd just lost the biggest opportunity of his life.

*B*en's mom was still up in the living room when he quietly closed the door, letting himself in just after midnight. He'd thought about hitting a bar, but he hadn't wanted to be around people.

She switched off the television and looked at him expectantly. "Where's your wife?"

He winced.

It was time.

"I signed divorce papers this morning." He settled onto the same couch he'd spent many a night sleeping on in the past fifteen months, three weeks, and four days. Mostly because he'd been too lazy to make the twenty-foot journey to his bedroom.

He'd told himself he was too tired after caring for his mom all day, but it wasn't fatigue.

Wasn't laziness either. Not really.

The aftereffects of shock, most likely. Coupled with stress and uncertainty and regrets.

And fear.

Definitely fear.

When had he become the guy who let fear guide his life?

"Divorce papers?" his mom said. "Why would that woman have brought you divorce papers? Doesn't she know what a catch you are? And I thought she was lovely. All those smiles and that spine of steel, not letting anything your girls said bother her at all. Takes one hell of a woman to *not* get in a catfight with her husband's girlfriends."

"Mom."

"I'm just saying, I didn't think you could do better than Emmanuelle, but Tarra...she's got spirit. You could use some spirit. Although I'm still mad you didn't tell me you were *married*. That's not the sort of thing a son should keep from his mother."

"It was a Vegas mistake." The part where he'd let her go without seeing if they could've had a real relationship being the mistake. Not the part where they got married.

He didn't know if he would've been a good husband. And the idea that he would've sacrificed his time with her to make all the same business decisions he had, to commit all his energy to professional success, made his gut ache in a way it hadn't since he'd walked away.

She was right.

He was too much work for a woman facing single motherhood.

"She didn't like you enough to fight for you?" his mom demanded.

"She deserves—"

"Oh, don't you start that with your mother. You're the catch of Coconut Bay, and not just because you're rich and handsome. You're charming too."

"Mom—"

"Everyone says so. Even when you're just being a lazy beach bum with your umbrellas, people like you."

He smiled. Leave it to his mother to ignore all his faults.

But that was what mothers were supposed to do, wasn't it?

Tarra would be an amazing mother. She'd be fun and spontaneous and loving and her kid was the luckiest kid on the entire planet to have her.

And her ex was a fool to let her go.

Maybe he hadn't let her go.

Or maybe she hadn't let him go, and she hid it well.

"I'm not going to marry Emmanuelle or Chloe or Nikita," he said. "I don't know if I'll ever marry anyone again, but if I do, it will *not* be one of them."

She waved a hand. "Oh, I know. They're all too high maintenance for you. But I thought you might actually try to find someone you *liked* if only to make me quit bringing them around."

"*Mom.*"

"Psh. If those three haven't figured out for themselves that you're not going to pick one of them, then they deserve what they're getting. And what girl wants a man whose mother arranges every date anyway? There's something not right about all three of them, you ask me."

He pinched his eyes shut.

Mothers. Mothers were a breed of their own.

"I'm going to bed," he told her. "You should too."

"I'll get there." She pointed to the TV. "But I need to watch and see how they flip this house first."

Ben took himself back to his bedroom and flopped into bed, where he didn't actually sleep.

Instead, he thought.

He thought about his life in California. About Lucas. About some of the uglier takeovers they'd been a part of. About the house he'd owned, the view he'd never appreciated, how nothing had ever been *enough*.

He thought about now, about Coconut Bay and its friendly residents, about his mother's backwards scheming, about the terror he'd felt when she'd come home with her diagnosis, about that tight band always around his chest, knowing he could be doing good somewhere in the world with his fat bank account, but terrified he'd spiral out of control again.

Because he'd had nothing else to live for.

Nothing but work.

Nothing *fun* since that day he'd run into Tarra every time he turned around in a Vegas casino, until he invited her to join him for a Venetian gondola ride, then invited her back to his room, the laughter, the sex, the *joy*.

He'd asked her to marry him because he'd wanted her joy.

And he'd let her go because he hadn't had a right to it.

Not when he was worried she wouldn't fit into his corporate lifestyle. When he put his job ahead of her.

He hadn't deserved her.

And why was he any better now?

After a long sleepless night, he was up with the sun. He hit the beach, hoping he'd catch her on another morning walk, but she wasn't there. And her car wasn't in the carport beneath her condo. And when he dashed up the stairs, he found the owner's cleaning crew already sweeping through.

She was gone.

Almost as though she'd never been there at all.

But she'd left something behind.

She'd left just enough of her behind to give him hope, and the courage, that he could finally figure out what he wanted to be when he grew up.

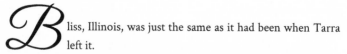liss, Illinois, was just the same as it had been when Tarra left it.

Giant wedding cake statue that could be seen a mile away? Yep.

Midafternoon shoppers clogging The Aisle, the main street in town where out-of-town brides came for everything they could possibly need for their weddings? Yep.

The scent of wedding cake lingering in the air, coupled with the banner reminding everyone that Knot Fest was rapidly approaching? Oh, yes.

It was all there.

Even the little house where she was currently living with Cinna, her baby sister, looked exactly the same as it had when she left. In theory, her sister Pepper lived here too, except Pepper had basically moved in with her boyfriend next door, which meant all Pepper did was pay the mortgage and pester Cinna for rent.

Tarra got a pass.

For now.

She shoved her key in the lock, twisted the front door handle, and pushed into the cozy living room.

Pepper and Tony leaped apart on the couch.

Tarra put a hand to the side of her face, blocking her view while she headed to the steps. "I see nothing, I hear nothing. Carry on."

"You're home early!" Pepper said brightly.

Too brightly. Like she was covering for the fact that Tony had his hand up her shirt two seconds ago.

Which was completely unnecessary. They were two consenting adults in love. Of course he should have his hand up her shirt.

"He signed the papers. I came home," Tarra said. Dang it, her voice was wobbling. Not good.

"Oh, honey," Pepper said softly.

And that was all it took. The dam burst, and Tarra erupted in tears.

The ugly tears. The splotchy-faced, gasping-for-breath, snotty-nosed kind of tears.

Pepper tackled her in a hug.

Tony headed for the kitchen.

And Tarra babbled.

"So sweet... So different... But the same... I should've stayed... I couldn't stay..."

"Slow down, slow down." Pepper guided her to the comfy easy chair in the corner under the lighthouse prints on the wall.

Lighthouses.

Ben had wanted to take her to climb the lighthouse in Coconut Bay.

Tarra sobbed harder.

She shouldn't have left him. He was hurting. Lonely. Lost. "He needed a friend," she told Pepper between sobs and gasps, "and I just *left* him."

By the time she'd gotten the whole story out—from finding Ben at the water parade, to getting soaked, to dinner with his mom and the harem, to him rescuing her from the seagulls, to him signing the papers, to their amazing day of playing tourist in Coconut Bay, Tony was back with hot chocolate chip cookies and a mug of peppermint tea.

Because she'd lived here long enough that Pepper's pizza-making boyfriend knew she liked hot chocolate chip cookies with peppermint tea.

Ben didn't know that.

But her sister's boyfriend did.

Tony ducked back into the kitchen.

Probably because he was a smart man.

"It's not your job to fix Ben," Pepper said softly while Tarra sipped her tea.

"But who else is going to do it?"

"You can't adopt men like other people adopt dogs. He has to *want* to figure out what to do with his life. You can't do that for him."

She knew that.

She did.

So why did she feel like *she* was the thing he could've done with the rest of his life?

He'd told her he was interested. He knew she was pregnant with another man's baby. He'd held his hand over her belly while her little pumpkin seed kicked for the first time last night.

But she'd tried to be what Jack had needed her to be too, and when she'd needed *him*, he'd bailed.

Saving her from the seagulls wasn't the same as holding her hand through labor, spending sleepless nights with a colicky baby, holding her when she cried because her baby was starting kindergarten and growing up too fast.

And she knew he could do those things—look what he'd done for his mom through her treatments.

But she didn't know if he'd do them for *her*.

"He's the reason I have Naughtea," she whispered. "He inspired me when we were in Vegas. He was so smart, and so together, and he liked *me*. He believed in *me*. He made me believe in me too. And I didn't tell him."

"That was ten years ago," Pepper said softly. "And you never even told us you got married. Was he really that special?"

The baby fluttered a kick in her belly, and she softly stroked her baby bump. "I was afraid if I told you, it would lose the magic," she confessed. "Because it *was* magic. For three days, we just...we *fit*." She swiped at her eyes. "I know it's silly. It was three days. The magic would've evaporated."

Pepper studied her closely.

Like she knew better.

Tarra could find magic in a pile of mud. She'd kept her optimism even when things had been tense with Jack. She'd stayed positive when she had failures and struggles when she was starting Naughtea.

She could've kept the magic in her relationship with Ben.

Magic was what she did best.

But she couldn't find Ben's path for him.

No matter how much she wanted to.

He had to want it for himself.

And she needed to concentrate on her baby. Ben could help himself. The baby, though—the baby needed her.

"Anyway, it's over now," she said. "I'll drop the paperwork off with my lawyer in the morning, and I'll officially, formally, be unmarried again."

"Oh, honey," Pepper said.

Tears were normal.

She was pregnant. And hormonal. And now, newly divorced.

Tears were completely normal.

*B*en's harem was right on time.

Or, what counted as *on time* around here. Nikita was two minutes early, Emmanuelle punctual down to the second, and Chloe would undoubtedly make her arrival seven minutes late, as she always did.

"I thought this was a date," Emmanuelle said with a frown at Nikita when she approached the table at Janie Mae's.

"It is," Nikita answered for him.

With a bit more sting in her voice than she'd had a week ago.

This wasn't going to be pleasant, but it was necessary. "Have a seat. Diet Coke's on the way."

Emmanuelle was more glowery than usual.

Chloe might be eleven minutes late just to make a statement.

He'd roll with it.

Tarra had been right. He needed to tell these three the truth.

And he should've done it months ago.

No, check that.

He should've never let himself get entangled with them to begin with. He'd been letting life live him instead of the other way around, and that needed to stop.

Today.

Nikita and Emmanuelle studied him while their server delivered the drinks Ben had ordered for the table. "No umbrella duty today?" Emmanuelle asked.

"Nope." He didn't care enough about umbrella duty on the beach to keep the job. It was time to let another beach bum take it over.

"Oh. My. God." Chloe screeched to a halt at their table, *early*, which was mildly discomfiting. "You're dumping us, aren't you?"

"Of course he's not," Emmanuelle sniffed. "His Vegas hooker is gone."

"She's *not* a hooker," Ben growled.

"She wasn't really your wife either," Nikita pointed out. "You've been here for like two years and haven't gone anywhere, and we know you slept with that divorced woman who was *finding herself* in Sariela's art studio last summer."

"I'm dumping you all," Ben announced.

Better to just pull the bandage off fast, right?

And it was fast.

So fast, he didn't see the Diet Coke coming until it stung his eyes. The people behind him shrieked.

The cold hit of a virgin piña colada followed, right on his forehead, dripping down his nose and into his crotch. Then something fizzled over his head.

Root beer.

Out of a bottle.

Glugging into his hair. Slowly. Intentionally.

He suppressed a sigh.

He'd earned this.

The three of them were shrieking, calling him names, insulting his manhood, the usual when breaking up with a woman, except times three, because he hadn't bothered to stop this in the first place.

He'd earned this.

So he let them have their say. Took some ketchup to the chest. Salt sprinkled in his hair.

Management came running. Other customers whispered and pointed. Probably filming the circus that was his dating life, because this was the good stuff for social media.

Especially when Chloe snagged a whole cooked snapper off a passing server's tray and walloped him on the ear with it. "And that's for giving my mother ideas!" she shrieked.

Which was really the least of his crimes.

"Why aren't you fighting this?" Emmanuelle demanded while she flung raw oyster meat at his head.

"Not worth it," he answered.

Which was the wrong thing to say.

Clearly.

Because when half the staff at Janie Mae's finally subdued his harem—none of whom he'd slept with, because apparently he'd still had *some* sense of self-preservation the last fifteen months, four weeks, and however many days—and when he was finally able to slip out of the oyster bar with what was left of his dignity, he had more food, condiments, drinks, and seafood shells stuck to his person than most people could eat in a week.

The manager followed behind him, mopping up the mess as he went.

"Probably you shouldn't come back in here for a while," she said.

"I won't," he promised. "Send me a bill for the mess. Probably should've done that in private."

"Don't feel too bad. Gatorbait posted the whole thing to Facebook, and it's already been shared over a hundred times in the last five minutes. Not so bad for business in the long run. But it'll take a while for those three to get over this. I meant you should lie low."

Lie low.

He could do that.

In fact, after he broke the news to his mom, he was going to do one better.

_T_ he divorce papers were taunting Tarra.

  It had been six days since she got back, and she hadn't dropped them off with her lawyer yet.

 She needed to. And she could claim she'd been busy. But she just hadn't wanted to.

 There was something so final in filing the paperwork.

 Ben hadn't texted or called. So apparently he wasn't broken up about her leaving, and he'd probably be glad to have the real, final, filed and certified paperwork in hand.

 But every time the baby kicked, she remembered sitting there in Coconut Bay, with Ben's hand on her stomach, knowing he couldn't possibly feel the little flutters, but his face had lit with wonder anyway.

 He'd had that same look when he'd asked her to marry him in Vegas.

 They'd hooked up the night before, spent a fun morning first at an overpriced breakfast buffet, and then headed up to the Eiffel Tower observation deck. She didn't even remember what she'd said, but whatever it was had prompted him to turn and look at her—_look_ at her, like he was seeing through her skin, through her bones, to the heartbeat in the very center of her soul, and he'd said _marry me._

Just like that.

And the words hadn't prompted fear. Or laughter. Or even disbelief.

No, the two little words had made something deep inside her click into place. Like *this* was what her entire life had been leading up to.

To finding *him*—smart, funny, ambitious, kind, and just as smitten with her as she was with him.

His proposal had been lightning striking.

Only if Elvis is there, she'd replied, and two hours later, they were hitched.

Easily the craziest, most spontaneous thing she'd ever done.

And she hadn't regretted a moment of it.

But clearly he had.

I'll call you, he'd said after they left the lawyer's office.

But of course he never had.

She'd deleted his number a few years later, because she'd needed to put an end to the fantasies and move on with her life.

And now here she was again, after spending less than thirty-six hours with him, wondering if he'd ever call.

"Your tea's cold." Cinna, her baby sister, leaned across the curved silver bar at Suckers, the bar their brother, CJ, ran here in Bliss. She was pulling a Saturday afternoon shift, and all of the usual Bliss gang was gathered here for a late lunch.

"I like it cold," she lied to Cinna.

"Don't be obnoxious. That's my job." Cinna had the red hair, green eyes, and full leprechaun personality that only half their siblings shared, and most days Tarra didn't mind, since she was part mischief herself, but today, much like all of this week, she was just plain irritated.

"And you do it so well," Pepper said.

Where Tarra had brought in her own tea for lunch, Pepper had brought in her own pizza. And Kimmie Kincaid had brought in two dozen cupcakes along with her twin infants.

CJ had eyed them all and threatened to toss them all out, but he'd been overruled when Natalie, his wife, had pounced on the bakery box and claimed a turtle cupcake for herself.

Plus, this was the normal slow time in the bar, and the only people in here—for the most part—were a core group of locals. CJ and Nat and their two boys, Nat's sister Lindsey and her husband and baby, their best friends Mikey and Dahlia and *their* baby, plus Kimmie and Josh and their twins. Pepper was flying solo since Tony was short-staffed at his pizza place today.

See?

Tarra wasn't alone.

She had her friends. And her baby would have lots of friends too.

She sighed and sipped at her cold tea while Kimmie and Lindsey compared their babies' sleeping habits. It was a conversation she should listen to, except she had enough nieces—and two nephews now —to know that every baby was different.

The door behind her opened, and she straightened while she watched the scene unfold in the mirror behind the bar. Maybe Ben—no.

No, Max Gregory and his girlfriend, Merry, were walking in. Merry's bright eyes were lit, and she was whispering a mile a minute.

Not unusual.

She wrote children's books, and she was always whispering about plot points to Max. They were adorable. And she was obviously inspired today.

"Look at you two," Cinna called. "Max, did you let her spy on people on the Aisle again today?"

"No, there was a guy going into Tony's place with a massive bouquet of teabags," Merry replied. "It got me thinking of everything else you could make a bouquet out of, and how many of them could fly."

Tarra's heart leapt in her throat.

Cinna snorted. "Teabags are for losers. Fresh tea in infusers is where it's at, but—"

Tarra didn't hear whatever else Cinna had to say, because she was leaping off her stool. "Pepper. Call Tony. *Call Tony.*"

Before Pepper could move, the door opened again, and this time, a massive bouquet of teabags walked in.

Tarra's heart swelled so large it almost burst.

"No *way*," Cinna squeaked.

Tarra was halfway to the door when a face peeked around the bouquet of individually-wrapped teas on sticks, wrapped with a red bow.

Ben.

Ben.

His dark eyes met hers, and all the anxiety melted out of his features. "You are so pretty."

She gasped out a laugh.

"You're going to have to do better than that, buster, because my sister is *so* much more than a pretty face," Cinna said behind her.

"She's brilliant," Nat agreed.

"And super successful," Kimmie added.

"And one of the nicest people I've ever known," Merry chimed in.

"Sshh!" Tarra hissed at all of them.

"Not a chance."

Ben smiled, Tarra stopped in front of him, and she fell.

She just fell. "You're here."

"Well, *you're* here." He held out the goofy tea bouquet. "Can I take you out for a cupcake? I hear there's a really amazing bakery downtown."

"I already brought the cupcakes here," Kimmie said.

"And you'd have to take all of us with you if you tried to walk out of here with Tarra alone right now," Cinna added.

Tarra sent her baby sister a *shut up* glare. "You'll wake up with shaving cream in your ears if you don't *shush.*"

"I'm so glad the troops are here. You're in no condition to be alone with a guy who's left you twice."

Tarra sighed. "Ben, meet Cinna and the troops. Cinna, leave Ben alone. Troops, hold her back."

She almost added an apology, but there was a light in Ben's eyes that hadn't been there last weekend. And he seemed more amused than petrified. Or worried.

"You have troops," he said, a smile growing on his lips.

"I—yes. Apparently I do."

"Good."

"Good?"

"I like a challenge."

"You're not going to get that out of Tarra," Cinna said.

"Shut *up*," Nat said to her. "Don't tell him she's easy."

"He still has to go through us," Cinna replied.

"No, he doesn't," CJ said. "Provided this is the one she married. One less sister to worry about is a good thing."

"Oh, you would *not* let her go with just anybody," Nat chided.

"What are you doing here?" Tarra whispered. She couldn't take her eyes off him. He'd gotten a haircut. He was in a button-down shirt. He'd shaved. And he'd lost those tight lines at the edges of his eyes.

"I met a woman," he replied. "And I decided I wanted to get to know her better."

She meant to take the tea bouquet, but instead, suddenly her arms were around him, her face buried in the crook of his neck, breathing in the lingering scent of beach mixed with fresh cornfield air. "This isn't simple, Ben. It's—"

"Worth it," he finished. "I know what I want to be when I grow up, Tarra. I want to be yours."

Her heart was about to pound out of her chest. "But—"

"I want to be your friend. I want to be your lover. I want to be your sounding board. I want to be everything you'll let me be. Wherever you are. However you'll have me."

"We hardly know each other." Which wasn't an objection she

would've had if she wasn't pregnant, and she couldn't deny it. But she *was* pregnant, which did complicate everything.

"Three dates, Tarra. Let me take you on three dates. Nothing has ever felt as right as you do, and I'm done being the fool who lets you get away."

Her friends' voices faded away as she reached up to kiss him.

All her fears dissolved, her apprehension faded, and that *click* happened again.

Her life, shifting into place. Her baby fluttering in her belly. Ben's lips teasing hers, his hands gripping her hips. "I missed you," he whispered between kisses.

"I missed you too."

"You took my heart with you when you left."

"I didn't want to leave. And I haven't given my lawyers the papers yet. I didn't want us to be over. But I didn't know if you—"

His grip tightened around her, and his eyes squeezed shut while he dropped his forehead against hers. "God, Tarra. I don't know if I'll ever deserve you, but I'm damn good at working my ass off for things I want. And I want to be worthy of all your light and joy and happiness. I want to *earn* the right to love you."

"Okay, I approve," Kimmie announced.

Tarra laughed, and Ben smiled at her.

"I'm taking a wait-and-see approach," Dahlia announced.

One of the babies squealed.

"What happens at the end of our three dates?" Tarra asked.

"I jump through hoops to make you happy enough to agree to a fourth."

"And where are you going to live?"

"Bought a house a few blocks away."

Her eyes bulged. "You bought a *house*?"

His grin turned sheepish. "I'm very determined when I have a goal."

"We could crash and burn," she whispered.

He shook his head. "I've crashed and burned before. This? You and me? We won't. There's too much *right*. And I'll move heaven and earth before I let you down. There's nothing—*nothing*—more important to me than making sure you and the baby are happy and healthy and loved."

The baby wasn't even his, and he already loved her more than her own biological father.

Tarra buried her face in his neck again.

She'd always been one to leap. This was the biggest leap of all, because she wasn't just leaping for herself.

But she couldn't resist Ben. She never could. And she didn't want to.

"Three dates," she agreed. "With an option on a lifetime."

He hugged her tighter. "Thank you," he choked out. "Tarra, you're —I—just *thank you*. I promise I won't let you down. Both of you."

Two weeks ago, she'd been setting up a trip to forever sever this man from her life.

Now, she couldn't imagine the future without him.

Life was funny sometimes.

And the rest of the time—times like today—it was simply perfect.

EPILOGUE

*O*ne year to the day after Ben's world finally found its axis, he was once again sitting in a beach chair surveying the water parade route.

But today, instead of a can of beer, he had a bottle of milk. And instead of being alone, his wife and baby were by his side.

He reached over and tilted Maya's hat to keep her whole face in the shade while Tarra finished rubbing baby-safe sunscreen on her chubby arms. They were farther back on the parade route than he'd been last year, and though they'd gotten squirted a few times, Maya hadn't objected.

If anything, she'd seemed delighted.

His sweet girl had her mother's sense of adventure.

"Ben! Benji! Oh my god, I didn't think you were coming *with a baby*." Emmanuelle stopped beside their chair, armed to the teeth with Super Soakers and water cannons strapped to her body. She was dragging along a wide-eyed guy in loafers, khakis, and a button-down plaid shirt who apparently hadn't gotten the memo about today's events.

Or possibly she was testing her latest candidate for Mr. Emmanuelle Genevieve Jones-Beaumont.

"She loves the water," Ben replied.

"And the fire trucks," Tarra added. She passed Maya to Ben. He offered her a bottle, and she latched on with both chubby hands and sucked it into her mouth. She was on the verge of crawling and had been sitting up unassisted for a couple weeks. If her friends back home in Bliss were anything to go by, she'd be unstoppable in approximately ten days.

"And visiting her Granny Betty," Ben's mom added as she stepped out of a nearby store carrying three stuffed bags.

Ben spied a stuffed plush lobster on top, and he wondered how many new suitcases they'd need to buy to get everything home next week.

"This is Mark," Emmanuelle announced.

"And this is Larry," Chloe said, approaching from their other side.

Nikita wasn't around—yet—though it was probably only a matter of time.

"We're planning a Fourth of July wedding," Emmanuelle said.

"Ours is Halloween," Chloe added.

Both men looked at each other and gulped.

"Married life is the best," Ben told them both. "I mean, after the first ten years."

Tarra tipped her head back and laughed. His mom swatted him on the shoulder. "Benjamin Anthony Garcia, *shame on you*."

Maya's bottom lip wobbled around her bottle, and her eyes went wet.

"Careful, Granny Betty," he warned. "Daddy's girl doesn't like it when people are mean to Daddy."

His mom *hmph*ed, but she was smiling. If he'd thought she was fully recovered a year ago, she was unstoppable now. She'd spent as much time in Bliss since Maya was born as she'd spent here in Coconut Bay, and she'd been going full-steam with everything she did.

But mostly with being a grandma.

Tarra's phone dinged six times. Ben glanced at her, she rolled her eyes, and they both laughed again.

Undoubtedly the Blue sisters in another one of their epic group text messages.

Her sisters were crazy. But they were also loyal and tight, and he loved how much they watched out for each other.

And how much they watched out for him too.

Sometimes.

Sometimes CJ or Basil or one of the brothers-in-law had to come to his rescue before he fully realized he'd gotten in trouble with the Blue women. And trouble wasn't something a man wanted to be in with the Blue women.

But being part of such a large family was still the icing on the cake of being Tarra's husband.

For real, this time.

They'd torn up the divorce papers, but they'd also had another wedding this spring. A small event—by Bliss standards—that they pulled together spur of the moment with pizza and cupcakes and ice cream and a vow renewal with all of their closest friends and family.

"Oh, look, here comes the fire truck!" Tarra squealed.

That was his wife. Still loving the hell out of every bit of life, finding the joy in the little things.

She'd helped find the joy in him too.

No, she *was* his joy.

His reason for waking up smiling every morning.

His inspiration for using his fortune to help struggling business owners in Bliss. There weren't many, but he'd found the professional pride he'd been missing without the overwhelming stress.

And then there was the Tarra factor.

She kept him from falling down the overworked businessman well.

She was the balance he'd been missing.

If anything, he had to pull *her* back from working too many hours.

Hadn't seen that coming.

"Look, Maya!" She leaned over and squeezed the baby's foot. "See the fire truck?"

Maya squealed behind her bottle and pumped her legs.

"Does Daddy's princess want a fire truck?" Ben asked her.

She pumped her legs harder.

Tarra laughed. "You are *not* buying her a fire truck."

"A *toy* fire truck."

His indignation was completely fake, and he knew she knew it. If Maya wanted a full-size fire truck, he'd have one in their front yard in half a day.

"Larry bought me a Corvette," Chloe announced.

Emmanuelle's left eye bulged. "Mark took me to Paris."

"Ben brought Kimmie Cakes with us when we left Bliss," Tarra said.

"And you didn't share any with Granny Betty?" His mom put a hand to her heart. "Benjamin. Give that baby to her mother. I'm going to drench you."

"Ah—"

"Honey, I'd save you, but I have a bad feeling that would just get all three of us soaked," Tarra whispered as she deftly lifted Maya out of his arms and dashed into the nearest store.

As soon as they were gone, his mom unloaded a Super Soaker on him.

Emmanuelle and Chloe fired water cannons.

Mark and Larry exchanged glances and dashed after Tarra.

But while Ben was lunging for the diaper bag, hoping there was at least a rubber ducky he could fill with water and squeeze at *someone*, a ruckus exploded from the store, and seven Blue women came streaming out, all of them firing water guns and cannons and flinging buckets.

All of them aiming at Ben.

All of them in swimsuits.

"Catch!" Tarra called.

She tossed him a Super Soaker, which he barely snatched before Cinna grabbed it, and he spun in a circle, shooting them all back.

Everyone was shrieking and laughing, Tarra and Maya included. The fire truck reached them, and its water hose drenched them all.

Once it turned the corner, Tarra snuck back out of the shop, Maya giggling and clapping on her hip. "Sorry," she whispered, going up to kiss him on the cheek. "They made me promise not to tell they were coming."

He flung an arm around his girls. "That's okay. I know where they live."

"We know where you live too, Mr. Stay-at-home Dad," Cinna said.

"Mm," was all he said back.

Because he didn't half-ass anything. Including prank wars with family.

And some things were best left for surprises. Especially with the Blue family.

Tarra was studying him like she knew exactly what he was thinking.

Which she probably did.

She'd always understood him, like their souls were linked puzzle pieces. He'd quit questioning how it happened, and these days, he just enjoyed his life.

Tarra's smile was growing. "I love you, you crazy man," she said.

"Not as much as I love you."

"Is that a challenge?"

He grinned at his wife. "Nah. Just the truth."

They were both laughing when the next parade truck launched a massive spray of water over all of them.

Maya squealed, Tarra's sisters shrieked, and Ben just smiled.

He was one lucky man.

The End.

ABOUT THE AUTHOR

Jamie Farrell is the alter ego for *USA Today* Bestselling romantic comedy author Pippa Grant. She believes love, laughter, and bacon are the most powerful forces in the universe. When she's not writing, she's raising her three hilariously unpredictable children with her real-life hero.

Visit Jamie's website at:
www.JamieFarrellBooks.com

THE COMPLETE JAMIE FARRELL BOOK LIST

The Misfit Brides Series

Blissed

Matched

Smittened

Sugared

Merried

Spiced

Unhitched

The Officers' Ex-Wives Club Series

Her Rebel Heart

Southern Fried Blues

JAMIE FARRELL'S PIPPA GRANT TITLES:

The Girl Band Series

Mister McHottie

Stud in the Stacks

Rockaway Bride

The Hero and the Hacktivist

The Thrusters Hockey Series

The Pilot and the Puck-Up

Royally Pucked

Beauty and the Beefcake

Charming as Puck

I Pucking Love You

The Bro Code Series

Flirting with the Frenemy

America's Geekheart

Liar, Liar, Hearts on Fire

The Hot Mess and the Heartthrob

Copper Valley Fireballs Series

Jock Blocked

Real Fake Love

The Grumpy Player Next Door

Standalones

Master Baker *(Bro Code Spin-Off)*

Hot Heir *(Royally Pucked Spin-Off)*

Exes and Ho Ho Hos

The Bluewater Billionaires Series

The Price of Scandal by Lucy Score

The Mogul and the Muscle by Claire Kingsley

Wild Open Hearts by Kathryn Nolan

Crazy for Loving You by Pippa Grant

Co-Written with Lili Valente

Hosed

Hammered

Hitched

Humbugged

Printed in the USA
CPSIA information can be obtained
at www.ICGtesting.com
CBHW032137120724
11511CB00011B/117

9 781955 930079